The Nubivagants

By Ethan Furman

Illustrations by Doan Trang

Published by Stone Mountain Publishing
Littleton, CO

Library of Congress Control Number: 2017900735
Furman, Ethan, Author
The Nubivagants
Ethan Furman

ISBN: 978-0-6928353-9-5

JUVENILE FICTION / FANTASY & MAGIC

QUANTITY PURCHASES: Schools, companies, professional groups, clubs, and other organizations may qualify for special terms when ordering quantities of this title.

For information, email ethanfurman@gmail.com

This book is printed in the United States of America

Published by Stone Mountain Publishing
Littleton, CO

To Mom & Dad, the best parents in the world...

And the Sky.

PART I: THE GROUND

Ethan Furman

1

You never forget the day you think you're going to die. Most people, if they're lucky, never have a day like that – or if they do, it's right at the very end of their lives, on the day they actually do die. Some people who lead particularly dangerous or adventurous lives may have a few of these days – lots, even – and they're all very terrifying experiences they never, ever forget. But even for these daredevils, those days usually come after they've grown up and decided to become soldiers or firefighters or skydiving instructors. They are adults doing dangerous adult things.

For young Matthew Mitchell, however, he had the unfortunate experience of being absolutely certain he was going to die when he was only eleven years old.

2

Before I tell you about this frightening and very life-altering event, perhaps a little background information is in order to help explain how Matthew got himself into such a predicament. To do that, we need to go all the way back to when Matthew was first born.

Well, maybe not *quite* that far back; only just about a week or so after he was born. Matthew's parents, Daniel and Allison Mitchell, had brought him home to their quaint little two-bedroom house in the quiet town of Tiburon, California – which is just a stone's throw away from the Golden Gate Bridge, across the bay from San Francisco. You see, that's when his parents first discovered there was one extremely interesting quality Matthew had that made him very, very different from your average, ordinary, everyday baby.

Little Matthew had a tendency to float.

"Float" may not be the right word, exactly. It was more like "hover." Meaning, when left to his own devices, his tiny body would quiver and twitch ever so slightly, as if a small pulse of electricity had zapped him. Then, ever so slightly, he would rise up off of the crib mattress, or his changing table, or wherever he happened to be lying at the time, and hover there in the air.

The first few times it happened, no one even noticed. Unless you were specifically looking for a space between baby Matthew's body and the surface he had been resting upon, you'd be forgiven for overlooking it.

Of course, Matthew's special condition could not be hidden forever. Eventually, someone looked at Matthew, looked away, then did a double-take and spit out her coffee as she became the first person to officially witness Matthew's floating.

Interestingly enough, that person was not Matthew's mother or father, the people who looked at him every day. Instead, it was Allison's good friend Eileen, her old college roommate. Eileen came over to meet the new baby, and after the initial cooing and oohing and aahing over him had died down, she began chatting with Allison, enjoying her nice cup of Italian roast coffee. And that's when she looked over to find Matthew floating about a half inch off the baby mat where he had been lying on the floor just a second earlier.

Eileen gasped, then let out a little yelp. "What is it, what's—" Allison started to ask, but once she turned and saw what Eileen was gawking at, there was really no reason to finish asking her question. Allison's eyes went wide. She stood up slowly, very nervous, and in a high pitched, frightened voice, called out to her husband, who was in the kitchen, unwrapping a stick of string cheese. "Daniel! Daniel come in here right away!" she shrieked breathlessly.

Daniel hurried into the living room to see his wife pointing at their newborn child. He looked down at his son and Daniel's eyes, too, bugged out of his face more than they ever had in his life. Not only that, but his jaw dropped down lower than it had ever before dropped. In one single second, Daniel's face set two individual all-time records, one for eye-bugging and one for jaw-dropping. (If there was a way to measure spine-tingling, he very well may have set that record too.) Slowly, he walked over to where Matthew was sleeping soundly, suspended in mid-air. Well, not mid-air, actually. More like very low-air, since he was just barely above his mat. He knelt down beside him, and after a moment of looking him over, reached out his hands to touch him. "Daniel!" Allison whisper-shouted. "Don't!"

"It's okay," Daniel said, his tone of voice indicating he had little confidence in what he had just said. But his hands continued stretching towards the baby. They slid underneath him, and pressed gently up on his

back. And then as the two women watched intently without so much as breathing, Daniel Mitchell simply plucked his sleeping son up out of the air and held him against his chest, just like he'd done dozens of times already in the boy's short life.

Daniel broke into a wide grin. "It's okay," he said again, this time more sure of himself. Allison allowed a shrill, short laugh to escape from her throat as she put a sweaty palm to her chest. Eileen, on the other hand, feigned a tight-lip smile; she was still very much unsure of how to react to this floating baby situation. She had no children of her own, but she still suspected this sort of thing was not exactly normal.

After a moment, Daniel gently set little Matthew back down on the mat, where his eyes slowly opened. He gazed up and looked at everyone, then let out a contented little gurgle as he sleepily scratched his nose. And then, without warning, he simply rose right up off the mat again, hovering in the air about a half-inch above it.

"Oh my god," Allison whispered. Daniel very cautiously reached for his baby boy again, but this time put his hand on Matthew's chest and gently pushed him back down to the mat. There he stayed for another few seconds before floating back up again. Once more, Daniel pushed him back down, and again, he floated back up, this time breaking into a smile and an adorable little laugh. Matthew seemed to rather like this game.

Daniel and Allison looked at each other. It was the first time they realized their son was truly extraordinary.

3

Now, it's sort of a lot to take in, coming to terms with the fact that your brand new baby has a tendency to defy the law of gravity. You don't just get used to that sort of thing overnight.

And believe me, Daniel and Allison tried. They spent most of that first night after this discovery in Matthew's room, standing above his crib, staring at him while he slept. Once in awhile they would crouch down, peer through the slats of the crib and eyeball the tiny gap between their child and the mattress. They would mutter words like "amazing" and "unbelievable." Then they would stand back up and just keep watching. They didn't even realize they'd been standing there all night, as the sky outside turned from black to purple to blue.

Finally, at just after seven o'clock the next morning, Matthew opened his little grey eyes, saw his parents staring down at him, and made a sleepy little gurgling noise. Allison and Daniel turned and looked at each other, the first time they'd looked at anything else besides their son in hours. "I think we should take him to the doctor," Allison said.

About an hour later, the Mitchells found themselves in the office of Dr. Bell, the man who had helped bring Matthew into the world. He was a little white-haired man with a trim little beard and little spectacles – in fact, everything about him was little. Everything except his voice, that is, which was booming and boisterous.

"The Mitchells!" he cried, as if he hadn't seen them in years. "What brings you back so soon?"

Daniel hadn't wanted to tell Dr. Bell's receptionist why they were coming in when he'd made the appointment on the phone, because he didn't want her to think he was crazy. He had just said it was urgent.

Now that they were here, however, Daniel and Allison still weren't really sure how to answer. They looked at each other (they had traded quite a few of these looks over the past 24 hours), and in this latest look it must have been somehow decided that Daniel be the one to explain why they were here.

"Well, Doctor," he began. "It's Matthew."

"What about him?" Dr. Bell asked, eyeing the baby boy. "He looks pretty healthy to me." Indeed, Matthew was relaxing comfortably in one of those snuggly pouches Allison had strapped to her chest, looking around at his surroundings curiously.

"Well he is, he is," stammered Daniel. "It's just that...well, yesterday we discovered that he...he floats."

"I'm sorry, what did you say?" Dr. Bell leaned forward slightly as if he hadn't really heard the words Daniel had just uttered to him. Daniel looked to Allison for help.

"He...floats," she repeated to Dr. Bell, without really expanding on her husband's original statement.

Dr. Bell squinted his eyes behind the thin frames of his glasses. "What do you mean, he floats?"

"I mean...well, look," Daniel said. He reached over and gently lifted Matthew out of his snuggle pouch, then placed him down on top of Dr. Bell's big wooden desk. After a moment, he took his hands off the baby and backed away.

Dr. Bell looked down at Matthew, thoroughly confused. "Daniel, I don't understand what you're..." This was one of the few sentences Dr. Bell started which he never finished. Because as he was in the middle of saying it, Matthew proceeded to rise up to his usual hovering altitude of about half an inch and stopped. Then he shook one of his little hands around and put a finger in his nose.

The doctor sat motionless, mouth agape, staring at Matthew for at least three minutes. That may not seem like a long time to you, but I assure you, it's a pretty good stretch to sit and stare at something, especially if other people are watching you.

"Dr. Bell?" Daniel asked after the first minute.

"Dr. Bell?" Allison asked after the second minute.

"Dr. Bell?!" they both asked together, a bit louder, after the third minute. This time, the doctor finally raised his head and tore his gaze away from the floating baby, looking over at the parents. He spoke in a soft, parched voice that sounded as if it had dried out in the desert sun.

He said, "I think we should run some tests."

4

Minutes later, the four of them were in a clean, white room, with Matthew positioned on an examination table. As Daniel and Allison looked on nervously, Dr. Bell shined a light in little Matthew's eyes. He stuck a thermometer in his ear. He tapped a small rubber mallet against his left knee, then his right. He listened to his heartbeat through a stethoscope. When the doctor concluded that everything seemed normal from these evaluations, he moved on to some more extensive tests, tests that had Daniel and Allison standing by and watching with their arms folded tightly, almost sick with worry for their newborn son.

Dr. Bell drew blood from the baby's little heel; the prick of the needle into his skin caused him to wail in pain and made Allison feel like throwing up. The boy was then placed inside a large, scary looking machine that looked like a giant tube, which took x-rays of his body. Sensors were stuck to his forehead to monitor his brain waves. He was even given a bottle of purple goo to drink that Dr. Bell said was supposed to taste like raspberry but was actually quite bitter and tart, and more like raspberry's creepy stepsister.

In the end, after all the tests were finished and evaluated over and over again by Dr. Bell, he came to the conclusion that there was absolutely nothing out of the ordinary about the infant, and certainly nothing that medically explained his tendency to levitate in the air. It was baffling and it was frustrating. There were simply no answers, not one, to the enormously intriguing question as to why Matthew was the way he was. And Dr. Bell was not someone who was comfortable being unable to find answers to enormously intriguing questions. Being a man of science, it made him feel quite anxious and uneasy.

"I'm sorry," the troubled doctor told Daniel and Allison when they came back to get the results of Matthew's many tests. "I simply don't know what's wrong with your son."

5

Whether something was "wrong" with baby Matthew or not, Dr. Bell had decided there was nothing really to be done, other than keep a very close eye on him. Everyone was left feeling highly unsatisfied with this lack of a solution, but what choice did they have? The only thing Dr. Bell could do for Daniel and Allison was give them an important piece of advice, advice that would dictate how they raised their son, and led to the very extraordinary events of the rest of Matthew's life.

"Listen," he said, his voice lowering to just above a whisper, even though they were alone in his office with the door shut. "I wouldn't tell anyone about this if I were you."

"Why not?" asked Allison, her voice giving away her slight alarm.

"Well, it's just better to be on the safe side," said Dr. Bell. "Your son's...condition...is very unusual, very unusual indeed. It's like nothing I've ever seen before, and I don't understand it one bit. And people..." He stopped, unsure of what exactly he was trying to say. "People tend to be frightened of the unusual, of what they don't understand. Sometimes...it brings out their darker sides."

As nervous as they thought they were when Matthew was undergoing all those tests, Dr. Bell's mysterious warning made his parents that much more uneasy. And so, with nothing more to be said, they thanked the good doctor and took their baby home. They didn't quite understand what Dr. Bell meant about the unusual bringing out people's "darker sides."

Eventually, they would.

6

After the visit to the doctor and all the tests and all the worrying, life in the Mitchell home actually settled into a somewhat normal routine. It took some getting used to, but after a couple months, Daniel and Allison became more and more comfortable with the fact that their son did not obey the law of gravity, until it simply became a part of their everyday lives.

Matthew continued growing into a healthy, happy little boy, and he learned how to move around in the air quite well. Instead of learning to crawl, like most babies, he taught himself to move his arms and legs as if he was swimming. It was slow and clumsy at first, but before long he figured out how to propel himself forward. After a few months, he was pushing himself off the walls, and was soon gliding and zipping and zooming about the house. He could even manage to thrust himself a bit higher up into the air for a few seconds, before whatever law of physics Matthew's body followed brought him back down to his regular floating level, which was also changing. When he was just barely born, Matthew floated only about half an inch off the ground. But as he got older and larger, he gradually began putting more and more space between himself and the Earth beneath him.

Allison first noticed this escalation about six weeks after they had seen Dr. Bell. She and Daniel had been watching a nature program on television in the living room, and Matthew was hovering above the carpet in front of them, playing with some plastic blocks. At one point he dropped a block, as babies tend to do, and made his way down to the floor to pick it up, upon which he drifted right back up into the air again.

While Daniel was focused on the feeding habits of hammerhead sharks, Allison had been observing the block-dropping episode play out on the carpet. "Daniel," she said, nudging her husband in his side with her foot. "Look. Doesn't he seem higher than before?"

Daniel peeled his gaze away from the TV and looked at his son. "Higher?" he asked, as if he didn't know what the word meant.

"Yes, higher," Allison repeated. "He used to float just a little smidge off the floor, like that much." She held her thumb and forefinger close together, a tiny gap between them. "But look at him now! He's, like, a good three inches up in the air."

Daniel studied his son, happily knocking the blocks together, until one fell again, perfectly illustrating Allison's point. "You're right," Daniel conceded. "He is getting higher." He looked at his wife, not at all happy about this discovery. He sighed wearily and closed his eyes, sinking down into the couch pillows. "Great," he said.

7

The discovery that Matthew was gradually gaining height as he grew older was not a joyful one for his mom and dad. You see, even as they got used to his floating and worried about it a little bit less, they both secretly held out hope that, over time, it would somehow correct itself, and Matthew would eventually return to earth and exist on the ground, just like everyone else.

As it turned out, precisely the opposite was happening. The older he got, the higher he levitated. When he was six months old, he was roughly six inches above ground. At a year, when most babies are learning how to walk, Matthew was swimming in the air around the house at about a foot off the ground.

This became more and more of a problem, because the more they thought about it, the more Daniel and Allison were intent on following Dr. Bell's advice of hiding Matthew's floating from the rest of the world. They were nervous, you see, that people may indeed be frightened by it, and they didn't like thinking about what that could lead to. At the very least, they wanted to avoid their child drawing a bunch of unwanted attention.

At first, it was easy. Babies are often restrained by something anyway: a high chair when they are eating, or a stroller when their mothers take them out for a walk, or someone holding them in their arms while fawning over them. So even floating babies seem quite normal in these everyday restraints.

But as they get older, babies naturally earn more opportunities to exist in the world without being constantly monitored or held down. And it was no different with Matthew.

When his parents took him to the park, for instance, it didn't seem fair for them to keep him in his stroller when all the other babies were free to crawl around on the grass and explore. To protect Matthew's secret, they would go to great pains to make sure they were in a shady, secluded area of the park, away from other people where no one would notice if, when they undid his restraints, he would rise up into the air and hover around above their picnic blanket. Once in awhile someone might happen to walk by, in which case one of them would very quickly snatch their baby out of the air and pretend like they were simply holding him. Occasionally, they would be a split second too late, and the passerby would do a double take, convinced they had just seen a baby suspended in midair. But always, that person would simply shake their head, knowing their eyes must have played a trick on them. Because, of course, everybody knows babies don't simply float in midair.

Interestingly enough, however, there was one place where little Matthew did not float: the bathtub.

Allison was giving Matthew his very first bath. She filled the little white plastic tub with warm water, and after testing the temperature herself, picked him up by the armpits and gently held his body under the surface to get him nice and wet.

Then she let go, fully expecting Matthew to rise up out of the water and hover his usual few inches above the surface. Instead, Matthew's entire tiny body rose to the surface of the water...and then stayed right there, bobbing horizontally as if he were an inflatable plastic inner tube. It must have been a soothing sensation for the boy, because after a few minutes of floating in the warm water, he fell right to sleep.

Keeping an eye on him the whole time, Allison's damp fingers dialed her husband's name on her cell phone. Her voice sounded thick as she explained this new revelation.

Daniel was intrigued but not comforted by the news. He didn't really see how it made anything better, aside from not having to worry about Matthew drowning – which was one of the few things they never worried about in the first place.

"Maybe we should move into a houseboat and just keep him tethered to the bow," he suggested jokingly. Allison was not amused.

8

For the most part, Daniel and Allison became quite skilled at protecting Matthew's secret. But the longer it went on, the more difficult it became.

When he was about a year old, they went through a period in which they tried to "ground him," in the most literal sense, by tying little weights to his shoes. The weights were somewhat of a success at first, as they prevented Matthew from floating up to his usual height. Encouraged, his parents began trying to teach him how to walk, one of them holding him down by pressing on his shoulders, while the other moved his legs in a walking fashion across the floor. But Matthew did not like these walking lessons at all; he was uncomfortable being held down and having his legs moved for him in this unnatural way. He was too young to understand what they were trying to do, and he would whine and cry after a few minutes of it, until finally they would give up, frustrated, and let go. Matthew would plop down and frantically pull at the foreign objects tied to his feet, his tantrums becoming more and more hysterical At that point his parents would remove the weights, and Matthew would promptly float back up to his standard altitude, his sobs subsiding, relieved to be free once again.

As the weeks grew into months, Matthew rose gradually higher into the air, becoming quite accustomed to living his life up there. Leaving the house with him became more and more of an ordeal. Things his mom and dad had never before given a second thought to had now suddenly become stressful matters of life and death.

Just a few days after his second birthday, Allison was talking to her mother on the phone in the kitchen. Matthew was floating around a few feet away, flipping through a book about dinosaurs. He was so engrossed in the pictures of brontosauruses and velociraptors, and Allison was so

engrossed in her conversation about the flat tire she had endured that morning, neither of them realized Matthew was hovering just a few inches beneath the ceiling fan.

Matthew had long hair for a boy, and when it was messy, it tended to stick almost straight up in some places. One of those tufts of sandy blonde hair was now drifting on end, right into the path of the high-powered ceiling fan, the blades of which began to *whap-whap-whap* the tuft repeatedly as Matthew ever-so-slowly floated towards it.

As Allison listened to her mother on the phone, she became aware of this strange sound, turned to locate the source of it, looked up, and was instantly petrified by what she saw. She shrieked, dropped her cell phone on the kitchen floor, yanked Matthew out of the air, and ran into the other room with him, unfairly scolding him for a near-accident that was in no way his fault. In addition, Allison's mother was annoyed, believing she had been rudely hung up on. Matthew was crying so hard, Allison didn't have the energy to care. It was an unpleasant episode for everyone involved.

Nevertheless, Daniel and Allison didn't really talk about Matthew's condition much, except to figure out how to avoid problems as they came up. (After the fan incident, for instance, Daniel removed the now-dangerous device from the ceiling.) But individually, privately, both of their minds were constantly thinking about little else other than what was going to become of their floating boy.

And so it went, until one night when they were lying in bed, lights off, both pretending to be asleep, but both very much awake with worry. That's when Allison finally sat up suddenly and switched the light on.

Daniel turned over to look at her, squinting. "Honey? Are you okay?" he asked.

"No," she said softly, her voice cracking with weariness and fright. "I'm not okay. Matthew's not okay."

Daniel sighed and rubbed his eyes. "I know," he agreed. "What do you think we should do?"

Allison looked at her husband. She opened her mouth to reply, even though she had absolutely no idea what to say...and just at that moment, the telephone rang. The loudness of the ring coupled with the quiet intensity of their conversation caused them both to jump a little bit. It was also after ten o'clock at night. Usually not too many people called this late, so they both looked at the phone, confused.

After the phone rang a second time, Daniel looked back at his wife, then picked up the phone and spoke into the receiver. "Hello?"

"Daniel!" cried a jolly voice on the other end of the line. "It's Dr. Bell. I hope I'm not calling too late?"

Daniel looked at Allison again as he responded. "No, not at all Dr. Bell." Allison's eyes widened at the mention of the doctor's name. "What's going on?"

"I've just been thinking about your little boy," Dr. Bell said. "To be honest, I haven't been able to get him out of my mind. Does he still...I mean, does he still have...um, does he..."

Daniel answered the question he knew the doctor couldn't find the proper words to ask. "Yes," he said. "He does. In fact, it seems to be getting worse." Allison nodded in agreement.

"I see," Dr. Bell responded, a bit eagerly. "Fascinating."

"That's one word for it," said Daniel glumly.

"Well, like I said, I've been thinking about this case a lot," the doctor said. "More than just thinking, actually. I may have come up with something to help your boy."

Daniel's face lit up. "You have? That's fantastic!"

Feeding off his excitement, Allison whispered "What? What?!"

Daniel raised a finger, silently telling her to wait a moment, which drove her crazy. "Why don't you come to my office in the morning, say, nine o'clock?" asked Dr. Bell. "We'll see what we can do."

"Absolutely. We'll be there. Can't wait! Thank you Dr. Bell," Daniel spit out all at once, every word climbing over the next to get out of his mouth and through the phone. Then he hung up and looked at Allison, who was waiting impatiently. He smiled. "He said he might have figured out how to help Matthew," he said.

Allison looked at him for a moment, processing this wonderful news, before letting out a tiny, shrill squeal of delight, and hugging her husband harder than she had in a long time.

9

Daniel and Allison had brought Matthew back to see Dr. Bell periodically after he was born. During the first year of any baby's life, there are many routine checkups to make sure everything is coming along as it should. In this respect, Matthew was no different. After every visit to Dr. Bell, he was given a clean bill of health. There was never anything the matter with him – except, of course, for that one thing.

Every time Dr. Bell checked Matthew out, he marveled at the way the boy hovered. His enchantment by Matthew's affinity to float increased with every physical exam the doctor performed. But in addition to his fascination, there was also a good deal of frustration. He was a very successful, very skilled doctor, you see. But in Matthew's case, it was literally the first time in his career he had come across a patient with a problem he could not correct, or even explain. This made him feel badly. He was almost ashamed every time Matthew left his office, because he knew how disappointed his parents must be that he could not help them.

That is why the doctor spent a lot of time thinking about the case of little Matthew Mitchell, as he told Daniel on the phone. In the office, at home, in the car, the grocery store, even in the bathtub – he puzzled over the boy nonstop.

And now, as he walked into his office at precisely nine o'clock on a crisp and sunny Thursday morning, the doctor beamed at Matthew and his parents, who were already sitting there waiting for him. The smile on his face told them he had finally reached some sort of answer.

"Ah, the Mitchells!" he greeted them as he sat down in his overstuffed brown leather chair behind his desk. "How are you this fine morning?"

"We're doing well, Dr. Bell," said Allison, who hadn't meant to rhyme.

Immediately Daniel followed up with "You said you might have found a way to help Matthew?" As if Dr. Bell had forgotten why he'd called late last night and told them to come in.

"Don't waste any time, do you Daniel?" Dr. Bell joked. Daniel was clearly in no mood for chitchat. He opened his mouth to speak again, but Dr. Bell held up his hand. He understood their urgency. "Let me start by saying that I have not come across anything that scientifically explains your son's condition, nor have I found a way to 'cure' it, for lack of a better term."

Daniel and Allison looked confused. "What do you mean?" asked Allison nervously.

"I'm saying that medically speaking, I know no more or less about what makes Matthew hover, or about how to make him stop hovering, than the last time you were here. Or the first time, for that matter," Dr. Bell said matter-of-factly.

Disappointment washed over Daniel and Allison's faces. They looked at each other. Daniel turned back to Dr. Bell, anger creeping into his voice. "But...but you said you could help him," he began.

"Yes, I believe I can," Dr. Bell replied. "You see, a good friend of mine is an inventor. Magnus Mapplethorpe. We went to medical school together hundreds of years ago..." Dr. Bell paused for any laughter that might come as a result of his little joke. There was none. "Anyway, he's a brilliant man. He's worked for the military, NASA, the airline industry, you name it. So old Mags is over for dinner the other night – he comes over a couple times a month – and we get to talking about your son's condition..."

"Wait a minute," Daniel interrupted abruptly. "I thought you told us not to tell anyone about this."

"Isn't there doctor-patient confidentiality or something?" added a concerned Allison.

The doctor stammered, clearly a bit embarrassed. "Yes. Well. I didn't mention your names or anything. Besides, Magnus is one of my oldest friends, very trustworthy." He looked at Matthew's parents, who still seemed somewhat disturbed by this betrayal. "Look, we'd had some wine, all right?" explained Dr. Bell. "A very nice red. I get a little loose-lipped after my second glass."

Daniel waved his hand, a little annoyed. "Go on," he said.

"Right. Anyway," continued Dr. Bell, "we're talking, and Mags reminded me that years ago, he had invented boots astronauts could use up on the moon or in outer space, where there's little to no gravity. The boots create a gravitational force that allows the astronauts to walk around as if they were on Earth."

Daniel and Allison listened, intrigued, as Matthew slept strapped down in his stroller next to them. "Okay," Daniel said. "And?"

"Well, after our conversation, old Mags went back to his lab. A week later I received a package here at the office. Inside that package...were these." Dr. Bell placed his medical bag on the desk in front of him, and removed what looked like a pair of baby booties. They weren't regular baby booties, though. Regular booties are soft and cottony, and are usually nice pleasing colors, like pink or yellow. These booties were thicker and made of some sort of shiny black plastic. They seemed very futuristic.

Daniel and Allison looked at the strange baby shoes. "What are they?" asked Allison.

"They're gravity booties!" Dr. Bell crowed proudly. "A series of sensors within the shoes align with the gravitational force of the Earth's surface, essentially serving to magnetize Matthew's feet to the ground. The sensors adapt to his walking habits, allowing for increases and decreases in gravitational pull as he walks around."

Allison and Daniel stared at the gravity booties, not quite sure what to make of all this. It was a lot of high-tech information to process. "Well..." said Daniel, but that was about as far as he got.

Allison managed a little better. "They certainly look...interesting," she said.

Their lack of excitement puzzled Dr. Bell. "This is an extremely advanced technological achievement we have here," he said. "I'm not sure you appreciate the genius and skill these took to create. Do you even understand what it is I'm saying to you?"

Daniel and Allison looked up from the booties to Dr. Bell expectantly, waiting for him to answer his own question.

"Matthew will be able to walk like a normal person!" he exclaimed.

10

After Dr. Bell said this, it immediately sunk into Daniel and Allison's heads that their son had the possibility of leading a somewhat normal life. They had come into the doctor's office with the expectation that he had found a way to cure Matthew's condition, or at the very least, discovered what was causing it. But in a way, the "gravity booties," as he had cleverly named this strange invention, were almost better.

The best-case scenario would be for Dr. Bell to discover the cause of the floating and, in turn, find a way to cure it and make Matthew just like every other gravity-obeying boy in the world. But that is an awfully tall order. If you go around expecting the best-case scenario to happen in every situation, you're setting yourself up for an awful lot of disappointment, I'm afraid.

On the other hand, a very bad scenario, if not the worst possible one, would be if Dr. Bell had told Daniel and Allison that yes, he had in fact discovered what it was within Matthew that caused him to disobey gravity, but that it was incurable and there was no hope for him to ever walk normally. That would have been devastating information to receive, despite providing the slim satisfaction of the case being closed, at least.

But these booties – ah, now this was actually some terrific news! This was a concrete solution to their problem! Once they got past the fact that they didn't actually know anything more about the cause of Matthew's floating, it dawned on them that it didn't matter! As long as the booties afforded Matthew the ability to live on the ground with every other human being, who really cared about anything else? It was what some people might call a "quick fix." And many times, quick fixes are the most attractive solutions to our problems.

As soon as Daniel and Allison managed to wrap their minds around the concept of the gravity booties, they too got excited. It wasn't long before little Matthew was awake and lying on Dr. Bell's desk. His old, low-tech toddler sneakers had been rudely tossed aside, and Dr. Bell was in the process of putting the exciting new gravity booties on his tiny feet. Once on, each booty was secured by an impressive strap with a silver buckle that crossed over the top of the shoe and, when pressed down upon firmly, produced a pleasing, confident sounding click that screamed "security."

In just a few minutes, both gravity booties were securely on Matthew's feet. Matthew seemed to share none of the excitement of the three adults surrounding him, and was content to stare up at them and suck away on his favorite binky. Nonetheless, after the click of the second booty buckle, Dr. Bell looked up at the boy's parents with a childlike smirk.

"What now?" asked Daniel, slightly anxious.

"Now," said Dr. Bell, "we turn them on." And with that, he reached down and pushed in a small black button on the inner heel of each gravity booty. The buttons were so unnoticeable that Daniel and Allison had not even...well, noticed them. But when the doctor pressed them, a tiny green light on each booty came to life and started blinking. Not only that, but the soles of Matthew's feet tilted forward just a smidge, towards the surface of Dr. Bell's desk, as if they were being pulled ever so slightly towards it.

Which, of course, they were. Just the sight of this minor movement of Matthew's feet was enough to cause smiles to burst out upon his parents' faces. "Whoa," Daniel said. "Cool."

But Dr. Bell wasn't finished yet. "Now let's stand him up," he said. Immediately, Daniel and Allison became nervous. This was a big moment. They each took a deep breath and nodded to Dr. Bell, signifying for him to proceed. The doctor nodded back, then carefully placed his hands under the toddler, and helped him up to a vertical state.

Because this was his first time, Dr. Bell was aware of the fact that he

couldn't just remove his hands and expect the boy to not fall over. So he kept one hand placed gently against his chest and his other near the small of his back, so that when Matthew inevitably started to tip one way or the other, the doctor could guide him back to a standing position – sort of like training wheels for a bicycle.

And just like riding a bike, after a few tips back and forth, Matthew got his bearings and – if only for just a second or two – stood on his own, right there on Dr. Bell's expensive wooden desk.

There was no floating. Not even a hint of it. For the very first time in his young life, Matthew Mitchell was obeying the law of gravity.

11

The three adults in the room were overjoyed with this breakthrough. Daniel bellowed a high-pitched "WHOO!!!" and grabbed his wife in a giant hug that lifted her right up off the ground. The happy mood of the room was contagious to Matthew, who giggled and clapped his hands together and shouted a "WHOO!!!" or two himself, even if he didn't really understand why they were celebrating.

Daniel shook Dr. Bell's hand heartily. "Thank you, Doctor," he gushed.

"You have no idea what this means to us, and to Matthew," added Allison. The doctor assured them it was his pleasure to be able to help them.

Then he gave them some instructions on the proper care and maintenance of the gravity booties, the details of which are probably about as interesting as skimming the instruction manual for your average microwave. "Let me know when he starts to outgrow them, and I'll have old Mags whip up another pair," said Dr. Bell.

Daniel and Allison grinned and thanked Dr. Bell again for everything he had done for them. But then the doctor adopted a more serious tone. "Now listen," he said. "For the first few weeks – months, even – you'll want to keep these booties on him most of the time, so he really adjusts to being on the ground. It's no good to only put them on outside the house, because that won't give him enough time to learn how to walk naturally. I can guarantee you he'll put up a fuss. They'll be uncomfortable for him. You'll be tempted to give him a break and take them off. Don't do it! When he's sleeping or in his highchair, fine. But when he's up and around, the gravity booties stay on his feet. Understand?"

Daniel and Allison understood. If there was one thing they were committed to, it was getting Matthew to learn how to walk right away. A little temper tantrum wasn't going to discourage them; they were in this for the long haul. After over two years of worry, they wanted nothing more than to have a normal, walking-on-the-ground little boy.

And so with that, Daniel and Allison thanked Dr. Bell again, who wished them well. Then they stood up, put their jackets on, and lowered Matthew to the floor. With each parent holding one of his hands, they slowly escorted him on his very first walk out of the doctor's office, out of the building, through the parking lot and to the car, which they got into and drove home.

12

Dr. Bell's warnings proved to be correct. It wasn't long before Matthew decided he didn't really care for the heavy gravity booties on his feet all the time, and if it was up to him, he'd kick them off and go right back to floating around barefoot. The problem with little children is they often believe things are up to them, when in fact they almost never are. This is the point at which they become upset, resulting in crying and screaming.

Thus, there was a lot of that over the next few weeks. Matthew made it very clear he was none too pleased to have his feet imprisoned in these strange shoes. As Dr. Bell suggested, his parents took off the booties when it was time for Matthew to go to bed. But the rest of the time, he whined and howled and sat on the floor, causing his parents quite a few headaches.

Nevertheless, they were determined to get through this and not give in to Matthew's protests. They worked diligently with their son, holding his hands and walking him all around the house and neighborhood. Why, they probably lost a few pounds each just from all the extra exercise they were getting.

In fact, they may have been trying a bit too hard. Even babies who naturally learn to walk without gravity booties don't usually have their parents giving them walking lessons. They just sort of stand up one day on their own and take a first step or two, which, if a parent is lucky, they will happen to witness and celebrate. There's an old saying that goes "You have to learn to crawl before you can walk." And since he had never crawled before, Matthew found it difficult to jump right into walking.

So Daniel and Allison eased up a bit, and decided to just let it happen more naturally. This proved to be wise. The gravity booties kept Matthew upright, so he progressed rather quickly, quicker than a normal child. After about a week of letting him figure things out on his own, he pushed himself up from a seated to a standing position all by himself.

He was on the kitchen floor one evening after dinner, playing with his favorite toy truck. Daniel and Allison were at the table, enjoying some coffee, discussing something the president had done that day. At one point, Allison looked down at her son and saw he was standing up straight, holding his toy, looking at them as if he was just as interested in the president as they were.

"Daniel!" Allison cried happily, interrupting him.

"What?" Daniel said, turning around. Seeing Matthew standing where he had just a moment ago been sitting, he grinned broadly. "Hey, little man! Look at you!"

Aware he had done something worthy of praise, Matthew smiled and replied, "Lookahme!" Then, without any hesitation, he raised his left little gravity booty-wearing foot in the air, and brought it down a few inches away. He wobbled for a second, in danger of losing his balance. But when he didn't fall, he looked back up at his parents again and laughed.

"He took a step!" Allison crowed, ecstatic. "Daniel, he took his first step! We saw it!"

"All right!" Daniel congratulated his little boy. "You did it, Matthew! Way to go!"

"Step!" Matthew cried happily. And then, for an encore, Matthew went right ahead and picked up his right leg, putting it down in front of his left...before finally losing his balance and falling down onto his butt. "Another one!" his dad pointed. "He took another step! That makes two of them. That's officially walking, right? That counts!" He looked to his wife for a ruling, as if she were a professional walking referee.

Allison smiled, beaming with pride. "It counts, honey. He officially walked."

"Yeah!!!" Daniel pumped his fist, leaned over and scooped Matthew up off the ground, kissing him on the cheek. Matthew squealed with delight. "I'm so proud of you. I'm so proud of my little walking man!" He passed off the boy to his mother, who took over showering him with kisses.

Daniel went to the refrigerator. "This calls for a celebration," he said, pulling out a bottle of champagne they had been saving for a special occasion. He popped the cork, causing Matthew to squeal again and clap his hands. Then Daniel poured a glass each for himself and Allison. He handed his wife her glass and raised his in a toast. "To Matthew's first steps in a normal life," he said proudly.

Allison had a tear of joy running down her cheek. "A normal life," she repeated softly, almost as if she were telling it to herself. "Cheers." And the two of them clinked their glasses together and took a sip of the best tasting champagne they ever had.

13

This next bit of the story goes by kind of quickly, like one of those sequences in a movie where you see a lot of time pass by, while uplifting music plays. I believe it's called a montage.

To put it simply, Matthew Mitchell began growing up. He went from being a toddler to a little boy. The gravity booties worked more or less as Dr. Bell had expected; eventually Matthew learned to walk around much like any other child. His mom and dad made sure he wore them as much as possible while he was awake, and even let him keep them on if he happened to fall asleep in them, just for good measure. Other than that, the only time he really had the booties off was when Allison gave him his bath, in which case he just floated right there on the surface of the water, making it rather easy for Allison to scrub him clean.

As Matthew and his feet grew bigger, Dr. Bell always had a replacement pair of gravity booties ready and waiting, compliments of the mysterious Magnus Mapplethorpe, whom the Mitchells never once met. The doctor charged Daniel and Allison a very reasonable price for the shoes – not much more than if they were just purchasing regular footwear for Matthew from a store in the mall.

And so, Matthew's childhood progressed. Weeks melted into months; months dissolved into years. As he grew older, he got used to walking, as if it was second nature to him – which it was, of course. He was much like a child born to parents who move to a new country. The child knows his native language, and speaks it at home with his family. But the more he is out and about in the world, the more he becomes comfortable with the language and culture and customs of his new land. So it was with Matthew and walking.

His parents enrolled him in preschool, where he quickly made friends, running around and playing with all the other children. At the age of five, he started kindergarten at the local public school. He instantly became one of his teacher's favorite students, because he was bright and got along well with everyone. He always got good grades, and as time passed, he learned to read, write and do math as he went from kindergarten to first grade, second grade, and so on.

Daniel and Allison couldn't have been happier or more proud of their boy. The fears they had about Matthew as a floating baby faded away, to the point where they barely thought about them anymore.

Of course, as he grew up, they had to make some specific choices about how to handle him. Every teacher, camp counselor, babysitter, or other person in charge of supervising him was instructed to never, under any circumstances, remove his special shoes – they were necessary to help with a unique foot condition he had. If the adult in question asked anything more about Matthew's foot condition – which they did, more often than one might suspect – Daniel and Allison would politely explain it was rare and complicated and, frankly, none of their business, and repeated that the shoes absolutely must remain on.

Because of this, as Matthew got older, he missed out on some things. He was not allowed to sleep over at friends' houses. He was not permitted to go swimming, or do anything that involved being barefoot – which, when you're a child, there's quite a bit of.

This pained the boy, but on many occasions his parents had long discussions with him about how he was different. "When you take off your shoes, you go up in the air," they told him. "We don't know why it happens. But no one else besides us can know about it."

"But why not? Why can't I tell anyone?" Matthew inquired.

Remembering the advice Dr. Bell had given them years ago, his mom and dad replied, "Because it makes you different. And sometimes people don't treat others nicely if they're different from themselves. Especially if they don't understand why."

14

Sadly, as he gradually became more aware of just how different he was, a change in Matthew's personality began taking place. He couldn't help but constantly think and wonder and worry about why he was so unlike all the other children he saw every day at school.

It didn't help that his parents were constantly reminding him of this fact. They were only trying to protect him, of course, but every time they told him he mustn't let anybody else know about his floating, Matthew felt as if there was something about him he should be ashamed of. In his own mind, he began to think "different" was the same thing as "worse."

Of course, nothing could be further from the truth. The truth is, the things that make people different are the same things that make them wonderful and special and uniquely individual. But perhaps Daniel and Allison, out of their instinct to protect their son, did not make this concept as clear to Matthew as they could have. Because little boys don't yet understand being different is perfectly all right. All they want is to fit in with everyone else.

But of course, Matthew did not fit in with the rest of the kids. And as time went on, this became more and more obvious. The other children began to question why he wore these funny-looking shoes he never took off. One time, in the third grade, after a particularly bad rainstorm, the school parking lot was completely caked with mud. When the children arrived for class, Matthew's teacher, Ms. Byrne, told them to please remove their shoes at the door, so as not to dirty the classroom floor.

Every student did as told, except Matthew. He stood in the doorway, watching the other kids sitting on the floor, removing their shoes without a second thought. "I...I can't take off my shoes," he said in a quiet, nervous voice, when one of them asked him what he was waiting for.

The others looked at him strangely. "Why not?" asked one girl.

"I just can't," Matthew replied, wanting nothing more than to be able to simply remove his muddy boots like everyone else.

"Do your feet stink or something?" teased an obnoxious little boy with red hair and freckles named Chad Gregory. Two other boys, Stu and Andy, who always hung around Chad and laughed at everything he said, quickly latched onto this idea, and started chanting, "Mat-thew's feet stink! Mat-thew's feet stink!" Within seconds, a group of children were chanting this cruel slogan in harmony, over and over again.

As Matthew's face got red and tears welled in his eyes, Ms. Byrne quickly came to his rescue. "Stop that this instant!" she chided the teasing children. "Go sit down and be quiet!" Ms. Byrne had of course been made aware of Matthew's "foot condition" and his need to keep his shoes on. So rather than make him take his gravity boots off, she fetched some paper towels and helped him clean the mud off them as much as they could.

But this only made it all the more humiliating for Matthew. As he and his teacher sat on the floor, futilely scrubbing the mud off his boots, he was painfully aware that every other kid in his class was sitting at his or her desk, perfectly shoeless, wondering what in the world was wrong with this strange boy.

It was moments such as this that came to define the unpleasant turn Matthew's childhood took.

15

The happy little boy Matthew started out as began to disappear. Because the other kids had labeled him somewhat of an oddity, nobody really wanted to play with him anymore, for fear they, too, might be thought of as strange. Matthew found himself without a single friend, which made him feel even worse about himself. And so he kept to himself at school, rather than risk further teasing by trying too hard to include himself with the other children. It was a bitter cycle that left him feeling unhappy, alone, and even angry.

But that wasn't the only thing that bothered Matthew. You see, when he was wearing his gravity boots – which was pretty much all the time – he never, ever felt comfortable. Even though he had been wearing them since he was a toddler, there was always something unnatural about them. He couldn't put his finger on it, and probably wasn't even consciously aware of it. But walking around on the ground like everyone else just caused this...queasiness inside of him, like a little, irritating itch deep down in his stomach he could never scratch. It was almost like he and gravity were having a never-ending game of tug of war. I imagine it would be the same feeling a bird might feel if you clipped its wings and it could never fly again. Birds were born to fly. And Matthew, apparently, was born to float.

Meanwhile, at school, that nasty redheaded boy, Chad Gregory, had developed into quite the bully, and saw to it to hassle, harass and tease Matthew every chance he got. He was quite a bit bigger than Matthew, and as you might have guessed, he was one of those boys who liked to make fun of other kids to make himself feel like he was better than everybody – probably because deep down, he didn't feel all that great about who he was.

This character trait didn't earn him too many buddies, outside of his followers, Stu and Andy. Those two boys weren't too bright, and were about the only people on the planet who thought Chad was actually funny – although more likely they just figured out they *should* think he was funny, so they could stay on his good side. In any case, Chad was their leader. Whatever Chad wanted to do, they went along with it. And that included making fun of Matthew.

This happened fairly routinely, in fact. By the time they were in the fifth grade, when Matthew was eleven, he had actually gotten used to these unpleasant encounters, as their frequency began to desensitize him. Usually, he just put his head down and hoped for it to end as quickly as possible. His trick for accomplishing this, he had discovered, was to agree with whatever Chad and his henchmen were saying. If they called him a weirdo, he would simply reply, "You're right Chad, I am a weirdo." If they accused him of having stinky feet, he agreed, "Yup. They're the stinkiest feet in the world." Usually, this tactic would lead to the bullies becoming bored sooner, and they would wander off to make trouble somewhere else, leaving Matthew alone.

But one day, something different happened.

Matthew came to school to see a new girl in the classroom. When the bell rang, his teacher announced to the class that this girl's name was Penelope, and she had transferred to their school from Colorado. According to the teacher, Penelope's father had gotten a new job, and her family had to move to California.

A new kid arriving in the middle of the school year was certainly an exciting development. But this particular kid was even more exciting. You see, by all accounts, Penelope was very pretty. She had curly blonde hair, rosy cheeks and a very big, toothy smile. After the teacher introduced her, she stood up and grinned at her new classmates, and everyone could see a huge gaping hole in the middle of her mouth where she had just lost a baby tooth – which, she announced proudly, the Tooth Fairy had taken in exchange for five dollars. This immediately impressed the other children, none more than Matthew, who found himself instantly taken with her. Most kids have already lost their front baby teeth by Penelope's age, so Matthew found it made her smile that much more special, in a way.

At lunchtime after class that day, Penelope was sitting by herself out in the yard. Coincidentally, this was also how Matthew spent the majority of his lunchtimes. So after almost ten whole minutes of working up his nerve, Matthew took a deep breath, stood up, walked over and introduced himself.

"Hi," he said in a squeaky, tentative voice. "I'm Matthew."

Penelope looked up at him, flashing that toothless smile. "Hi Matthew," she replied, friendly. "I'm Penelope."

Matthew smiled back. He opened his mouth to continue the conversation...but was shocked to find it suddenly filled with a strange orange taste. In fact, it was all over his face, as well as his shirt. He wiped his eyes, only to see Chad – with Stu and Andy right behind him – laughing and holding a shaken up can of orange soda, which he was still spraying all over Matthew.

"You don't wanna be friends with this fruit loop!" Chad laughed evilly. "His feet stink! Why do you think he wears those weirdo shoes?"

Penelope didn't know what to make of this rude interruption. Some of the orange soda had gotten on her, too, and she quickly got up and ran off to the bathroom. But not before she glanced down at Matthew's feet.

She didn't mean anything by it, of course. She was just as flustered as Matthew was. But it didn't matter. She was gone. "Hahaha! Look, your stupid shoes scared her off, freak!" laughed Chad.

"Yeah, nice move, idiot!" chuckled Stu.

The three bullies stood there, laughing and high-fiving each other. Matthew's cheeks burned. Of all the times Chad had teased him, none made him feel as horrible as this one. He wanted to kill him, he wanted to punch him in the face a thousand times, but of course he couldn't. He wanted to run after Penelope and apologize, even though he hadn't done anything wrong. But he couldn't. She was in the girls' bathroom, and even if she hadn't been, he was too humiliated to do anything at all.

So instead, he just started crying. Then he stood up, grabbed his backpack, and went home.

16

Matthew's parents were quite surprised to see their son come home in the middle of the day, when he should have been at school. When they asked him what was going on, he immediately took his anger out on them. In his mind, they were to blame for his problems. They were the ones who had made him this way, they were the ones who had burdened him with this secret that made it impossible to explain himself to the other children, which caused them to exclude him.

"I don't want to wear these stupid boots anymore!" he wailed to his parents. "I hate them!"

"Matthew," his father replied wearily. "We've been over this. The boots are what keep you on the ground. You have to wear them, and that's that."

Matthew's mother noticed the ugly orange stain on his clothes. She reached out and felt his shirt. "Why are you all wet?" she asked, concerned. "What happened to you?"

"NOTHING!" Matthew shouted, very upset.

"Don't shout at your mother," Daniel said, sternly. "Now calm down and tell us what happened."

"Nothing," Matthew said quieter now, too embarrassed to go into detail about the orange soda incident. "Just...sometimes, other kids make fun of me. I don't have any friends." He started crying again, frustrated.

"You just need to try harder," Daniel said. He was frustrated himself, because he didn't know how to help his son, and he was sick of having the same conversation for what seemed like the hundredth time. "You need to toughen up a little bit, Matthew."

Matthew's eyes darkened. This suggestion, to "toughen up," made it seem to him that his dad was saying his troubles were his own fault, and could be solved so easily if only he made more of an effort. And that notion was so unfair and caused him to become so angry, he said something he had never said before.

"I hate you."

His mother gasped, shocked. His father looked at him, eyes going wide. "What did you just say to me?" he asked in a quiet but furious voice.

Matthew was scared. But somehow his fear only served to fuel his anger. The next time he spoke, he was surprised to find himself yelling.

"I hate you!" he shouted. "I hate you for making me this way! I wish I was never born! I'd rather be dead than have to keep living this way!" Before his parents could even respond, Matthew ran off to his room and slammed the door.

There is perhaps nothing more painful a child can say to a parent than those three words. Daniel and Allison never dreamed their son was capable of saying such a thing to them. In fact, Matthew himself didn't know he had those feelings inside him, not until that very moment. But sometimes, when you're hurting badly enough, the only thing you want is to hurt someone else.

17

Matthew stayed in his room the rest of the night. Allison knocked softly on his door at about 7:30 to ask him if he wanted to come downstairs for dinner, but he declined, simply muttering "I'm not hungry."

The next morning, Matthew came down dressed for school and wearing his gravity boots, just like he did every day. His parents were already in the kitchen, dressed and drinking coffee, just like they did every day. When Matthew said "Good morning," got himself a bowl of cereal and sat down at the kitchen table – just like he did every day – his parents looked at each other, not exactly sure how to react.

They hadn't had any idea what to expect, really. They weren't even sure if he would want to go to school, or if they should prepare themselves for another unpleasant incident. In fact, they were quietly wondering aloud to each other if they should go upstairs to check on him just a minute or two before he came into the kitchen.

But now Matthew was sitting there at the kitchen table, eating his cereal, as if it was just another day. Except whereas the three of them were usually upbeat and talkative in the morning, today the mood was tense. They could all feel it, a chilly thickness in the air around them.

Have you ever gotten into a fight with a close friend, or maybe a family member, and you simply didn't know how to act the next time you saw them? You're not quite as upset as you were before, but there's still that uncomfortable awkwardness about who should speak first, and what should be said? If so, you understand perfectly the mood of that morning's breakfast between Matthew and his parents.

"Good morning," his mom and dad both said, almost weirdly in unison, responding to their son's greeting. That was about as far as they got for a couple moments, after which Daniel improvised by asking lamely, "How'd you sleep?"

"Fine," Matthew said, without going into further detail. Another few seconds passed in silence. Inside, his mom started becoming upset all over again. She could feel her face getting hot. Maybe she was overwhelmed by the impossible task of protecting her son from the world. Maybe she was disappointed Matthew had not apologized for what he had said the day before. Either way, Allison was not a person who was good at hiding what she was feeling. She was the type who needed to get things off her chest.

So she sat down at the kitchen table across from her son. "Matthew," she said softly.

Matthew looked up at her from his cereal. "Yes?" he responded.

Allison glanced over at Daniel, who was quite curious himself as to what she was about to say. Then she looked back at Matthew. "Um...I think...I think after school today, when you get home...well, I think we should all..." She paused, trying to find the right word. "Talk," she finally finished. She looked up at her husband again, to see if he had anything helpful to add. He nodded in agreement. "Yeah," he said, lending support to his wife's suggestion. "You know, no big deal. The three of us will just...talk. Okay buddy?"

"Okay," said Matthew. He took the final bite of his cereal, then got up and put his bowl and spoon in the sink. He picked his backpack up off the floor, slipped the straps on his shoulders, and looked at his parents, who were watching his every move closely. "See you later," he said, then left the kitchen and, a moment later, the house.

18

Matthew, of course, had done a lot of thinking the night before. He had been upset by what Chad had done to him at school, sure. But to be honest, what his father had said to him made him about a thousand times angrier. His suggestion that he simply needed to "try harder" and "toughen up" was merely the match that lit the fuse to the growing powder keg inside of him.

It just wasn't fair, Matthew concluded. No other kid in his school, in the whole world, had to deal with this floating nonsense that burdened him. No other kid had to wear these ridiculous shoes he couldn't ever take off in front of people. No other kid had to keep a secret this big about themselves, unable to tell anyone else the most important thing about them. *Lucky me*, thought Matthew sarcastically, as he trudged down the sidewalk.

As he walked the mile and change to school, his thoughts turned back to the previous afternoon. He remembered yelling at his mom and dad, telling them he hated them, and blaming them for the way he was. He felt badly, because he didn't really hate them. He loved them, of course he loved them. They were his parents, and they had shown him nothing but love his entire life. You would have to be a real lousy brat, Matthew decided, or else have really horrible parents, not to love them. It was practically automatic.

Matthew sighed. For the first time, he put himself in his parents' shoes, which were more normal looking than his (even metaphorically), and realized how much he must have hurt their feelings. The more he thought about what he'd said, the worse he felt. He even thought about turning around and going home to apologize, to tell them he hadn't meant it, and that he loved them very much. But he couldn't do that; he'd be late to school, and besides, his dad had probably left for work by now anyway. So he decided he would do it as soon as he got home. His parents had said they wanted to talk to him, so he knew he would get his chance. By the time he got to school, he actually felt much better, knowing that by the day's end, he would make things right. Nobody in his life was more important to him than his parents. That was the first thing he planned on telling them when he got home.

Unfortunately, he never got that chance.

19

The day progressed uneventfully, for the most part. Matthew went to his classes, spent lunch and recess by himself (as usual), and even felt pretty good about his answers on a pop quiz in science. But unfortunately, he just couldn't quite make it through the day without this calm being destroyed.

Because as the final bell rang, and Matthew got up to go home and make up with his mom and dad, his eyes met Penelope's. He suddenly got very nervous, unsure of what she thought of him, or what he should do. But then, before he had a chance to do anything, something beautiful happened. She smiled at him.

Matthew's heart sung. All the embarrassment, all the frustration and anger and hurt he had been consumed with for the previous several hours – the previous several years, in fact – suddenly vanished. For a moment, at least, he was happy. And so he smiled back.

But as you may have guessed, Matthew's happiness didn't last long. You see, Chad had noticed this touching, heartfelt moment between Matthew and Penelope, and he didn't like it. It made him jealous – jealousy being another ugly characteristic of bullies who secretly don't like themselves very much. So he decided to ruin that moment for Matthew by flicking him in the back of his ear and whispering "Twerp!" into it as he walked past him.

Now, an ear-flick was relatively minor on the overall scale of bullying Matthew received at the hands of Chad Gregory. It didn't even actually hurt that much. Maybe because it was such an abrupt end to the brief moment of happiness he was experiencing, or maybe it was just the buildup of his lifetime of frustration finally erupting like a volcano. But whatever it was, something in Matthew snapped. And so he turned and pushed Chad as hard as he could.

No one in the world expected Matthew to do what he did – least of all Chad Gregory. Matthew himself didn't even expect himself to fight back against his longtime tormentor. So Chad was completely unprepared for this mighty push, and it sent him crashing into a desk, which broke under his considerable weight, then tumbling to the floor.

No one – not Matthew, not Penelope, not the other kids, not even the teacher – said a word. A freezing silence took over the room as Chad's eyes went wide, his face turned bright red, and he looked up at Matthew, trying to decide on which of a hundred ways to kill the boy.

Petrified, Matthew stared right back at Chad. For a moment, neither of them moved.

Then, Matthew ran.

20

He bolted right past Chad, still lying on the floor, just barely escaping the bully's arm as it shot out and tried to grab his leg. Matthew registered hearing Chad scream "GET HIM!!!" as he ran out the door and sprinted down the hallway, weaving around other students who were unaware one of their peers was fleeing for his life. Later on, more than one of Matthew's schoolmates would tell the police they thought they could hear him making a funny sound – sort of a high-pitched, distressed whining noise – though if you had asked him about it, Matthew would have no recollection of such a thing.

He ran out the front of the school, through the parking lot. Seeing nothing except for what was right in front of him, he ran across the street and narrowly avoided being hit by a car, which swerved violently. The man behind the wheel, an older gentleman with quick reflexes, was quite shaken up by having almost run over a little boy. (In fact, the incident would change the course of this man's life in a very deep and profound way...but that is an entirely different story, for another time.)

Matthew turned and ran down the sidewalk, continuing on for a good three or four minutes, until he came to a supermarket. The hustle and bustle of the cars and shoppers unnerved him; in fact, it downright freaked him out. So he turned and saw an alleyway, running alongside and behind the supermarket, and diverted his path down there.

Finally, the alley dead-ended with a locked chain-link fence. It was just as well. Matthew's heart felt like it was going to burst out of his chest. He needed to stop for a minute. He felt dizzy, and his vision became blurry. He realized it was because his eyes were full of tears. This is an incredibly bizarre feeling, if you've never experienced it – to suddenly gather you've been crying for who knows how long without having known it. Crying is usually the sort of thing you can feel coming on, even prepare for. If you're amongst company, you can probably stave it off for a couple seconds while you excuse yourself and get to someplace more private. But in this particular instance, Matthew's emotions were well ahead of his awareness.

And so the tears came, all at once, like a raging river bursting through a dam. Too weary to support himself on his own feet, he leaned up against one of the grimy green dumpsters in the alleyway behind the supermarket and slowly slid to the ground, heaving great big sobs of sadness.

It's okay, thought Matthew, trying to calm himself down. *It's okay, you're safe now, just pull yourself together and —*

"Hey weirdo!"

Matthew's head jerked up from where it had been positioned between his knees. His breath seized in his throat, putting an instant stop to his sobbing. He blinked his eyes a few times, enough for them to clear and allow him to see whose voice was addressing him so rudely.

It was Chad Gregory, of course. He was standing about twenty feet away, where the parking lot ended and the alleyway began, Stu and Andy on either side of him.

"Start saying your prayers, freak," Chad said, as he began walking slowly towards Matthew. "You just made the biggest mistake of your short life."

Matthew sat there, stuck to the ground as if he was in some terrible dream. As frightened as we was, he wouldn't have thought things could get any worse.

He was wrong.

21

"Look at him," one of Chad's tagalongs chortled (did it matter which?), as the bullies strode menacingly towards Matthew. "He's crying." The other Chadling laughed loudly, because that's what his feeble brain thought he was supposed to do.

"Why you crying, fruit loop?" laughed Chad. Matthew did not respond. "I'm the one who cut my arm on the desk." Chad held up his arm, showing Matthew a pretty decent-sized gash with dried blood crusted around it. For a second, Matthew actually felt proud of himself. "You don't see me crying, do you?"

Chad and his minions stopped, towering over Matthew sitting in front of the dumpster. "I asked you a question, dummy," said Chad, his voice lower and more threatening this time. "Why are you crying?"

Matthew looked down at the ground. He really didn't need this right now. He just wanted to disappear. He wasn't even afraid, really – just exhausted. In a small voice, he managed to get out, "Just leave me alone, Chad."

Chad laughed, cueing Stu and Andy to laugh as well. "Leave you alone? After what you just did? Oh, I don't think so. That wouldn't be very fair, would it?"

"Yeah," Stu or Andy replied. "That wouldn't be fair at all."

Matthew decided he didn't want to be picked on anymore at the moment. With an inner strength he didn't fully understand himself, he slowly stood up, wiping his face with his shirtsleeve. The three bullies were blocking him from going anywhere, so Matthew looked Chad in his dark, beady eyes. "Please get out of my way," he said softly. "I want to go home."

Chad stared right back at him for a long moment. "Then go," he finally said, in a low, scary voice.

Matthew held Chad's stare. Then he glanced at Stu and Andy. Nobody moved. Matthew took a deep breath and tried to push past Chad, who slapped him in the face with his open palm.

Matthew was stunned. All over again, his face burned hot with anger, his cheek stinging from where Chad had struck him. He looked at the bully with shock. If he had looked over at Stu or Andy, he would have noticed they, too, were surprised by Chad's action. They had not expected it. But Matthew's eyes were locked on Chad's.

Everything after that happened very quickly. Matthew made a sudden break for it, trying to shove Chad away from him so he could run away. But Chad was bigger, stronger and faster. As soon as Matthew's hands made contact with his chest, he grabbed the smaller boy's arms and wrestled him back down to the ground.

In a flash, he had Matthew pinned to the asphalt. Matthew was aware of the unsettling detail that he was getting dirt in his hair as Chad applied the weight of his body onto him.

"Grab his arms!" Chad screamed at Stu and Andy. "Help me hold him down!" Unprepared for this development, Stu and Andy looked at each other. They were unfamiliar with much else other than doing their leader's bidding, so after silently communicating with each other, they sprung into action, kneeling down onto the ground. Each of them grabbed one of Matthew's arms, keeping him flat on his back. Struggle as he might, he wasn't going anywhere.

Confident the other boys had him secured, Chad crawled over to Matthew's feet, which flailed around as he tried to get free. He grabbed one of his ankles out of the air, taking a closer look at Matthew's unusual gravity boot.

"I've always wondered about these weirdo shoes you wear," Chad said. "Let's take a closer look at them, shall we?" His fingers found the buckle, and he began pulling at it.

"NO!!!" shrieked Matthew helplessly. "Don't take it off! Leave me alone!"

But Chad did no such thing. He pulled at the buckle until it clicked open. The pressure of the gravity boot around Matthew's foot disappeared, and Chad was able to easily slip it off.

"PLEASE!!! Please Chad! Put my shoe back on!"

Chad ignored him, inspecting the unusual black boot. Now he was genuinely intrigued. "Why do you wear these all the time?" he wondered aloud. He turned and looked at Matthew writhing around on the ground. "What happens if you take them off?"

"Nothing!" Matthew screamed in despair. "Nothing happens! Please, let me go! Let me have my shoe back!"

"If nothing happens, then why are you freaking out about this shoe so much?" Chad asked – an admittedly good question. He looked at Stu and Andy, his face darkening. "Keep holding him."

Stu and Andy nodded, even though they were tiring, as Chad snatched Matthew's other ankle in mid-kick. This time, he noticed the blinking green light on the back of the boot. He stared at it, bewildered. "What the...?" he mused to himself.

Then he reached around the shoe, and in one quick motion, he ripped the buckle open. The light on the back of the shoe went dark, as Chad removed it from Matthew's foot.

Staring at the gravity boot he held in his hand, Chad stood up. He looked down at his two henchmen, holding the writhing, screaming, helpless boy down on the ground. "Let him go," he instructed.

Stu and Andy looked up at Chad for confirmation. He nodded. "Do it."

Matthew's eyes went wide with terror. He began breathing very heavily. "No. Wait—" he started to plead. But before he could say any more, his captors had released him, getting to their feet, themselves considerably tired out.

There was a brief moment where nothing happened. It probably seemed a lot longer to Matthew, who mistakenly thought a miracle was occurring.

But that moment quickly passed.

22

As Chad, Stu and Andy stood and watched, Matthew began levitating, inch after alarming inch of air separating him from the asphalt he had just spent the last few minutes uncomfortably pinned against.

"Holy crap," mumbled Chad softly. The three bullies were beyond stunned. Any number of adjectives could be used to describe what they were feeling: disbelief, confusion, excitement, and so on. No one word encompasses it all, so I may as well just make one up: disconcitement. Chad, Stu and Andy were experiencing mass disconcitement.

Matthew, on the other hand, was really only experiencing one feeling, and that was terror. He had never floated uncontrolled outdoors before; he always either wore his gravity boots, or had his parents' hands no more than a few inches from his body. And even that was when he was a baby, so he had no real recollection of those experiences.

"Help!" he cried. "Don't let me float away!" His head banged against the handle of the dumpster, which if he had been facing, he might have thought to grab onto. As it happened, his hands instead flew to his injured skull, as he drifted past what would ultimately be his best chance at avoiding his fate.

In typical mean kid fashion, Chad and his two servants did not help Matthew; in fact, they did not even attempt it. In their defense, this was not because they were purely evil; they were really just too shocked to move. So, being rooted to the ground in awe, their eyes and mouths gaping wide open – much the way Daniel and Allison's did the first time they witnessed Matthew's remarkable ability – Chad, Stu and Andy simply stared as Matthew floated up past the dumpster, crying out futilely for help.

His legs and arms flailing, Matthew drifted up towards the roof of the

supermarket. He managed to twist himself around, and with a couple powerful breaststrokes, he thrust himself up against its beige, hard surface. It was made of some sort of concrete, a bumpy stucco surface that offered nothing in the way of something to grab onto. So as Matthew's hands scrabbled frantically against the supermarket's outer wall, he continued upwards.

When he reached the roof, he was dismayed to discover that here, too, there was nothing for him to grab hold of. Many roofs have a drainpipe, or a raised edge of some sort that can come in handy if you're about to fall (usually down, but in this case, the fall was up, if the definition of the word "fall" permits such a thing). But for some unlucky reason, the roof of the supermarket had no such feature. It was just a flat roof, at a 90-degree angle to its wall, covered in little pebbly bits of gravel on top – totally worthless in terms of preventing an upward fall.

Matthew yelped as he rose up above the supermarket, reaching for it uselessly as he moved further and further away. He looked down and caught a glimpse of the three boys, staring dumbly up at him, becoming smaller with every second, their facial features disappearing into indistinguishable pink blobs.

Matthew rolled over, looking for something, anything to grab onto. He saw a tree towering over the back of the supermarket, one with long, thin branches and bright green leaves. He was maybe 15 or 20 feet away from the tree, and in a few more seconds, he would be above it. It seemed he was actually gaining speed the higher he went, although whether or not this was true or just his own perception, we'll never know. The only thing that mattered to Matthew in this moment was getting over to that tree.

Pumping his arms and legs furiously like an Olympic swimmer, Matthew powered his way through the air towards the tree. He was moving his limbs as fast as he could, but unfortunately for him, swimming in air is much more difficult than swimming in water. Water is thicker and provides more resistance, so the more energy you exert, the faster you go. Air is so thin, it's tough to generate any real speed by flapping your arms and legs. If Matthew had had wings, it might have been a different story. But alas, he was a boy, not a bird. It was going to be very close, whether he could get to the tree before he floated past it.

Amazingly, Matthew did reach the tree. In fact, stretching out his arm as far as it would go, he succeeded in grabbing hold of the absolute highest branch the tree had to offer, jutting up into the sky above all the others!

Matthew managed to grip this thin little branch just a few inches from its end point, and for an instant he was overjoyed, his heart bursting with relief and gratitude, as he thought he had saved himself. But because of his momentum, as well as the flimsiness of the branch, it was not able to support the weight of his body as he plummeted upwards into the sky. And so the branch snapped off in his hand, his joy vanishing, and up he went, with one less option for survival.

Matthew stared with disbelief at the useless twig he now held in his hand, then dropped it, looking around for something, anything else that could save him. And he saw it.

Directly above him, only a few feet away, in fact, was a power line. The distance between it and him was rapidly closing, so before he could think too much about it, he stuck out his hand to grab onto it.

But when his fingers first came into contact with the power line, he felt a tiny sting, a little zap of electricity that caused him to jerk his hand back instinctively. Now, while power lines are electrified, they are only dangerous to the touch if you are standing on another surface – like, say, a ladder – because the electricity then has someplace to go. However, if you are not "grounded" by anything, then the electricity has no place to get to. This is why birds are able to sit on power lines comfortably without getting electrocuted. And this was the same situation Matthew was currently in – he was in no danger of being shocked by the power line, since his body was not in contact with any other surface.

But being just a ten-year-old boy, Matthew might not have known this information. He may have thought there was a good chance that by touching the power line, he would be fried to a crisp. Even if he wasn't fully thinking about this possibility – because saving himself from floating off into space was his biggest priority at the moment – the notion of being zapped to death very well may have been present in the back of his mind.

So when he first touched the power line, and felt the very common, very minor shock of just regular old static electricity – the kind that causes even the bravest of us to yelp and pull our hands back – Matthew overreacted, mistaking this harmless shock as one much larger and more dangerous. And so instead of grabbing onto the line, he instinctively pulled his hand away from it.

This split-second was all that was necessary for him to lose his final chance at latching onto something that was attached to the Earth's surface. A moment later he was five feet above the power line, then ten, then twenty. The planet and everything on it was becoming smaller and smaller, as it faded away below him.

Matthew began praying this was a horrible dream, and any moment now, he would wake up, sweating but safe, and could go into his parents' room, tell them about his nightmare and curl up next to them for comfort. He closed his eyes tightly, hoping against hope that when he opened them again, it would be the middle of the night, and he would be at home in his bed.

But when Matthew did open his eyes a few seconds later, that was not the case. What he saw was a group of five or six squawking birds flying directly at him! Matthew screamed – something along the lines of "AAAAUUUUGGGHHHHH!!!!" – and the birds scattered at the last second, sparing themselves a collision with this strange creature, the likes of which they were used to encountering only down on the ground. Panicked and unable to breathe, Matthew looked up and saw he was approaching an enormous bank of white, fluffy clouds. He was extremely high now, with no chance whatsoever of reversing course.

This, of course, is where you first met Matthew, way back at the beginning of the story. He was sure, at this point, what his fate was going to be. He knew how it would all end. They say sometimes when people reach their final moments, a sense of calm comes over them, helping to ease them across to the other side – whatever that may be. But with the white fluffy clouds turning a scary, deathly gray color the closer he got to them, he experienced no such calm. As he closed his eyes, his mind losing consciousness, preparing itself for its grand finale, Matthew was as terrified as he had ever been in his whole life.

Ethan Furman

PART II: THE SKY

1

Matthew blinked his eyes open, but had to squint them shut again immediately. The light was nearly blinding, and he was completely disoriented.

A number of things had to be processed. First of all, the fact that he had woken up to begin with. As he was floating upwards into the sky and everything started going dark, Matthew's last thought was that surely he was about to die – in which case, of course, he would not have woken up, and would certainly not be having these thoughts now. So the very notion that he was once again conscious was kind of a big deal, and it took him a moment to move onto his next thought.

Which was: where was he? He was no longer moving; he was at rest. Before he got any further in the process of figuring things out, however, he heard voices.

"He's awake!" said one.

"Yeah, look! He's blinking his eyes!" said another.

"We can all see him, Liam," said a female voice. "We don't need a play-by-play."

"Okay, sorry," replied the previous voice – Liam, you can assume. "I'm just excited. Jeez, Pam."

Matthew, utterly confused and a bit frightened still, tried to look around. His eyes took a little while to adjust to the glaring light, but after some more blinking and squinting, he began to make out the silhouettes of people standing around him.

Slowly, he managed to push himself up onto his hands, into a position between lying down and sitting up, which greatly delighted the people whose voices surrounded him.

"There he goes!"

"Yay!"

"He looks alright! Y'alright, mate?"

Matthew did not register that someone was speaking to him directly. He was still too overwhelmed and confused by everything. After all, he had only been awake and aware he was still alive for less than a minute. He was not entirely prepared to have a conversation yet.

He gradually took in his surroundings, looking down to take in the surface he was laying on. It was soft, fluffy and white, as if he was nestled in an enormous cotton swab. His hands pushed down beneath him, sinking into the whiteness a bit, only to have it gently push them back up again. It was actually extremely comfortable, like the most luxurious bed you could imagine.

That's when it hit him: he wasn't floating! He wasn't wearing his gravity boots, and he wasn't floating! He was just laying there, in this cool, spongy white fluffiness, perfectly stable, just like a normal person! This exciting realization sharpened him up immediately, as the voices around him came more into focus, chattering on, one on top of the other:

"He's not responding."

"Maybe he's deaf."

"He's probably just in shock."

"Of course he is. Don't you remember how confused you were when you first arrived?"

"You were loads more confused than me."

"No I wasn't! You were a blubbering idiot!"

"Ya better get yer memory checked, mate, 'fore I wipe it clean for you."

"Oh ho! I dare you to try!"

"Will you two shut up! This kid's been here two minutes and you're already squabbling?!"

"Seriously. Can we focus on *him* right now?"

Matthew finally became aware that the surrounding voices were talking about him. He blinked slowly and carefully, trying to make out the faces in front of him.

There were five people – kids of differing ages – standing in a circle around him. An older teenaged boy with dark skin stood directly above him; a girl with frizzy hair and a face full of freckles stood next to that boy. Looking around, Matthew saw two skinny, pale boys a bit older than him who looked identical to each other. Finally, Matthew noticed a little girl (maybe about seven) with jet-black hair, olive skin and piercing green eyes, grinning from ear to ear.

"Who are you?" he asked, looking around at this group, his question directed at no particular one of them specifically.

The kids around him broke into large smiles, claps, and sounds of joy upon hearing Matthew's question. "He speaks!" cried one of the twin boys.

"I *told* you!" crowed the frizzy-haired girl in a nasally voice. "I *told* you he was fine. He just needed a minute to get his bearings!"

"Congratulations," said the other twin, rolling his eyes. "Pamela's right yet again."

"He's new!" screamed the little girl with delight. "I'm not the newest anymore!"

"That's right," the older teenaged boy said, ruffling her hair. "You've got seniority now."

"S-sorry," Matthew said tentatively. "But...who are you? Where am I?"

"Oh, my bad," said the older boy, kneeling down next to Matthew. "We're your new family," he said. "My name is Calvin." He held out his hand. "What's yours?"

"Matthew," replied Matthew, instinctively shaking Calvin's hand. "Matthew Mitchell."

"Well, Matthew," replied Calvin in a soft, reassuring voice. "There's

nothing to be afraid of. We'd like to welcome you with open arms to your new home. I think you're going to like it here very much. All of us do."

"But...where is here, exactly?" Matthew asked, studying this boy's dark, yet kind eyes.

Calvin smiled at him. "You're in the Sky."

"The Sky...?" Matthew repeated hesitantly. He looked down again. His hand clenched around a clump of the surface he was laying on, scooping up a handful of the wispy whiteness. Then he realized: it was a cloud. Another realization immediately hit him, one that chilled him right down to his core.

Perhaps he had not survived after all.

2

Matthew looked up at Calvin, and at the others staring down on him from above, the sun framing them in angelic bright light. "Am I...?" He couldn't even bring himself to say it, it sounded so preposterous and scary.

Calvin stared at him blankly, waiting for Matthew to complete his thought. Matthew took a deep breath to collect his words. "Am I...I mean, is this..." Matthew swallowed, forcing himself to ask his question, even though he wasn't at all sure he really wanted to know the answer. "Heaven?" he finally eked out in a tiny voice.

Everyone stared at him for a long moment. The silence was finally broken by one of the twins, who suddenly doubled over laughing, clutching his stomach with both hands. "He thinks he's dead!" the boy managed to belt out between guffaws. "He thinks he's died and gone to heaven!"

The boy's brother smacked him on the arm. "Give 'em a break, Pete. It's a perfectly reasonable conclusion to draw when you wake up in the clouds."

But this just made Pete laugh even harder. He fell onto the cloud and rolled around, howling with laughter. "I suppose that means all of us are dead as well!" he wailed with glee. "Lookit me! I'm a ghost, yeah?" (Pete and Liam both spoke in lilting Irish accents Matthew had only ever previously heard in movies.)

Matthew felt a bit relieved that the notion he was dead and now in some form of the afterlife was not only false, but also ridiculous – at least according to this Pete fellow. But he couldn't help but feel kind of embarrassed that this kid was having such a hearty laugh at his expense and confusion.

Calvin sensed Matthew's discomfort, and put his foot down squarely in

Pete's chest as he rolled around. "Ooof," Pete groaned, his laughter silenced as he sank down into the surface of the cloud a few inches.

"That's enough," said Calvin. "I seem to remember you being pretty freaked out when you first got here, too." He lifted his foot up.

"Why does everyone keep saying that?" asked Pete, getting back to his feet. "At least I didn't think I was dead."

"I'll explain it to him," said the frizzy-haired girl, "since you guys are so easily distracted." She plopped down next to Matthew. "Hi! I'm Pamela. Everyone calls me Pam."

"Hey," Matthew replied. "I'm Matthew."

"I know. You said that already." Matthew could already see how Pamela might rub some people the wrong way. She swooped her arm up above her head, making a dramatic attempt to show Matthew his surroundings in one large movement. "THIS is the Sky. The Sky is exactly what it sounds like. The five of us live up here in the clouds. We call ourselves the Nubivagants. And now it looks like you're the sixth member of this very exclusive group." She looked up at the others. "See? That's not so hard, is it?"

"The Nubi...what?" Matthew stammered.

"Nubivagants, mate," chirped Pete.

His twin brother Liam quickly followed up with an explanation. "Nubivagant is a word that means 'moving through the clouds.' And since we move through the clouds...we are the Nubivagants." He beamed at Matthew proudly.

"But I don't understand," Matthew spluttered, confused. "How did you all get here?"

"The same way you did, Matty," said Calvin.

For the first time, something impossible dawned on Matthew. "You mean..."

"Yer like us," said Pete, his demeanor more serious now. "And us, well...we're—"

"Like you," his bespectacled brother finished.

It took a moment for Matthew to understand what they meant. "You mean...you...you all float too?"

Pamela nodded matter-of-factly. "Yup," she said. "Being nubivagant is a very rare and special condition, reserved for very rare and special people. No one knows what causes it."

"Betcha thought you were the only one, eh mate?" said Pete.

Matthew nodded, stunned. Since he could remember, it never occurred to him there might be someone else like him. Even for a boy who floats, finding someone else who shares the same characteristic is something you have to see to believe. And Matthew had never seen anyone else who could do what he did, so he just assumed he was the only one.

Matthew's thoughts were interrupted by the sound of Calvin's voice. "We all did," explained Calvin. "Each of us thought we were the only ones. Well, except Pete and Liam, of course." He nodded at the teenaged twins, each with rust colored hair – Pete's spiked up like a rock star, the more straight-laced Liam's parted to one side smartly. They smiled the exact same smile at Matthew at the exact same time.

Matthew's head was spinning. He had so many questions, he couldn't organize his thoughts long enough to be able to get a single one out. It was as if all his inquiries were pushing and shoving each other to try and be the first one out of his mouth, and as a result, there was a big logjam, and none of them succeeded. Instead, he sat there dumbfounded.

In the end, one notion overpowered everything else, a concept that welled up from deep inside him. It rose from his feet all the way to his head, a warm, fizzy feeling that felt like carbonated butter flowing through his veins. When he finally found his voice, it came with tears brimming in his bright blue eyes, as he managed to speak this truth that seemed too good to be true.

"I'm not alone," he whispered, and the tears immediately began running from his eyes down his cheeks. But he was not crying the way he had the previous night, when he was so upset and angry that he told his parents he hated them. (How long ago that now seemed – an eternity!) No, these were tears of pure relief. And as Calvin knelt down and put his arm around him, the exhaustion of spending his first twelve years of life feeling isolated from the rest of mankind poured out and away from him, more and more in every individual tear. Matthew could actually feel his body become lighter – which is funny, since it was his very weightlessness that had weighed him down emotionally up until now.

And over and over again, he kept repeating the words: "I'm not alone."

3

Matthew had a good, hearty cry, which caused the other kids to tear up a little as well. For them, it brought back similar memories – both the pain of feeling lonely and strange, and the joy of realizing there were others like them. This was the joy Matthew was experiencing now, and they could feel his relief radiating off him in waves.

The little girl walked up to him and gave him a hug. "Don't cry," she said sweetly in a delicate Latin American accent. "Crying is sad. I hate sad."

Matthew laughed, hugging the girl back. "I'm sorry," he said. "There, I think I'm done now." He wiped his eyes, then rubbed his runny nose on his shirt sleeve – which resulted in a long, unsightly string of mucus connecting his wrist to his face.

The other kids reacted in disgusted horror. "Oh man!" shouted Liam.

"Gross!" shrieked Pam.

"This one's a bloody savage!" remarked Pete, as Calvin put his hand over his mouth, keeping his thoughts to himself.

Mortified, Matthew noticed his sleeve and plunged it down into the cloud by his side, out of sight. "Sorry," he said meekly. Only the young girl offered anything other than commentary. She reached down and scooped up a handful of the cloud Matthew was sitting on. Then, to Matthew's amazement, she squeezed and molded it into a compact, firm little wad, then used the cloud compress to wipe Matthew's nose.

Matthew was taken aback, but allowed the girl to clean his face. It felt very refreshing, like a little moist toilette you might get at a restaurant that serves baby back ribs. But it also had the most delightful scent of the freshest rain you've ever smelled in your life. "All clean," the girl said when she had finished.

Matthew breathed in deeply, immediately soothed. "Thank you so much," he said to the girl. "What's your name?"

"Antonella," she replied, her bright green eyes twinkling at her new friend.

"Thank you, Antonella. That was amazing. You can use the cloud as a tissue?"

"We use the clouds for everything," Pam said, as Antonella balled up the used wad and tossed it over her shoulder. Matthew watched as it fell down through the clouds behind her and disappeared.

"The cloud gives us everything we need," said Liam, pushing his glasses up the bridge of his nose, as he took a seat next to Matthew. "See?" Liam also scooped up a handful of cloud, putting it right into his mouth, where it melted almost instantly.

Matthew was shocked. "You eat it?!" he exclaimed.

"Course we do," his brother Pete quipped. "What else would we eat?"

"I don't know," Matthew said. "I hadn't really thought about it."

"It's water," said Liam, helping himself to another scoop. "And some other nutrients too, I think. We're not entirely sure. But it does the trick. And you can have as much as you like. It's not like we're going to run out anytime soon. Go ahead, try some!"

Matthew scooped up a little bit of cloud and licked it tentatively. It tasted even better than it smelled! Cool and with just a hint of flavor, it dissolved on his tongue as soon as he touched it, turning into beads of refreshing water that ran down his throat. Matthew stuffed the rest of his handful into his mouth, then immediately reached down and grabbed two more fistfuls. He hadn't realized how thirsty he was till he tasted the cloud!

Liam laughed. "Like it?" he asked.

"It's delicious!" Matthew said exuberantly. "What else do you use the clouds for?"

"The question is, what do we *not* use them for," Pam replied. "We sit in them, we sleep in them. We even make our clothes out of them!"

Matthew looked around. It wasn't until this very moment that he noticed how the other kids were dressed. Each of them was, in fact, wearing clouds for clothes! He hadn't noticed at first, what with everything else there was to take in. But sure enough, each Nubivagant was dressed in a unique white cloud garment.

He took a closer look at them all, amazed. Calvin wore pants and a t-shirt; Pete was sporting a vest while Liam wore shorts and a smart looking cloud blazer; Antonella was clad in a lovely sundress, and Pam was draped in a long, flowing gown that looked like an ancient Greek toga. Each piece of cloud-clothing was wispy and translucent and moved in the breeze; the garments themselves seemed to have a life of their own. "Wow," Matthew said, each moment in the Sky fascinating him more than the last.

"So," Pete said, taking a seat across from Matthew, sizing him up. "What's yer story, mate?"

"M-my story?" replied Matthew, a little nervous. Something about Pete's demeanor made him feel a bit intimidated. He almost reminded him of Chad in a way...acting tough, as if Matthew was some sort of threat to him.

"Yeah," said Pete. "Where ya from? How long ya been floatin'? How'd ya get 'ere? Y'know...yer story."

The rest of the kids took a seat in a circle, like a campfire without the fire, looking at their newest member. "Yeah, let's hear it," said Calvin. "Tell us about yourself, Matthew. Then we'll tell you our stories."

"Uh, okay," Matthew said. He was a bit surprised. He had never told "his story" to anyone before. His parents already knew everything there was to know about him, and he never told anyone else his secret. This was the first time in his life had he been asked to truly speak about himself.

But once he began talking, the words just poured out of him effortlessly, like water from a faucet. He told the Nubivagants about his mom and dad, and how he had floated ever since he could remember. He told them about how beautiful the town of Tiburon was. He told them about Dr. Bell, and how his friend Magnus had invented these gravity boots that allowed him to walk from a very young age.

"Whoa," Liam interrupted. "Gravity boots?! That's incredible! Why didn't I think of that?"

"Excuse me Liam, but who's telling the story?" scolded Pam. "You'll get your chance in a minute!"

"Alright, alright, sorry," said Liam, looking down. "It just sounds really cool. Gravity boots," he said again under his breath, impressed.

"Go on," said Pam, smiling sweetly at Matthew.

Matthew went on. He talked about how he actually came to hate the gravity boots, how he didn't really have any friends at school, because everyone thought he was some sort of weirdo. He told them about Chad and his two imbecilic sidekicks, and how they bullied him practically every day for years.

Then he told them about the new girl at school, and how he had mustered up the courage to talk to her, but Chad ruined everything by spraying orange soda on him. In a quiet voice, he recounted how he had taken out his anger on his parents, and that they told him the next morning – *this* morning – that they wanted to talk about everything when he got home from school today...but he never got the chance. Finally, he got to the awful conclusion, of how Chad and his cronies chased him down in that alley behind the grocery store, took his shoes, and watched him float away.

When he had finished his story, the circle was dead silent. Matthew looked around at the Nubivagants' faces, and they all looked quite stricken with sorrow. "Wow," Liam finally said. "That's a doozy, mate."

The other members of the group nodded in agreement. "Don't worry Matthew," said Calvin. "Those days are behind you now." He looked around at the others. "Okay, who wants to go next?"

4

"I'll go!" said Pamela, her hand shooting up in the air.

"Big surprise," muttered Pete, rolling his eyes and leaning back into the cozy little cloud-chair he had made for himself. In fact, the Nubivagants had all made themselves comfortable, shaping and molding the cloud around them into various pillows or chair formations they could relax into. Matthew watched the others shape the clouds to their liking within seconds, but then struggled to clump up handfuls of cloud into much of anything, really. After a few minutes, he hadn't produced much more than an unstable, lumpy blob he had a hard time staying upright in.

"Here, let me help you," Calvin said, who was relaxing next to him in a very comfy looking cloud version of a lounge chair. He crawled over and went to work, gathering up cloud tufts and packing them in against Matthew's body. After a couple minutes, he had a nice little cushion to lean against. Nothing fancy, but it did the trick. "Comfy?" he asked.

"Yes, thank you," he replied, a bit embarrassed.

"Don't worry, you'll get the hang of it in no time," Calvin smiled.

"Excuse me," said Pam, exasperated. "But I thought I was going to tell my story!"

"All right, all right, go ahead Pam," said Calvin, crawling back to his lounge chair. "Not like any of us is going anywhere."

"Thank you," Pamela said, dramatically clearing her throat. She began speaking in a high-pitched voice that was overly sweet but commanded attention. "Well – where to begin? My name is Pamela Finkelstein. I'm 13 years old, born in raised in New York City. Manhattan, okay? Not Brooklyn, not Long Island, not upstate, but New York City proper. You got it?"

"Uh, yeah," said Matthew, confused as to why this was such a big deal.

"New York City."

"Good. Anyway, I had a great childhood. Good friends, straight-A student, first-chair violin in the school orchestra..."

"Crikey, Pam, he don't need every detail," said Pete. "Just give 'em the headlines."

"These *are* my headlines," Pam shot back. "This is who I am. You can tell your story however you want. Right now I'm telling mine."

"Whatever," Pete sighed.

"Like I was saying," Pam turned back to Matthew. "Everything was going great. I mean, my parents got divorced when I was seven, but it was for the best. There was a lot of hostility. Much better now. You know what I'm saying?"

Matthew nodded, even though he really didn't.

"So I went back and forth between Mom and Dad. Kind of a hassle, but I actually liked having two bedrooms. I had a lot of decorating ideas. I'm very creative. Anyway. My parents had a summerhouse in the Hamptons. They kept it after the divorce, and just split time there. So one summer a few years ago, I was staying there with Mom and my little brother, Jimmy. And my favorite thing to do was, late at night, after everyone went to bed, I would go out into the backyard and look up at all the stars with this telescope my dad gave me for my seventh birthday." She held out her hand. In it was a small, silver telescope that glinted in the sunlight. Matthew stared at it, surprised.

"You can't really see too many stars in the city, because all the lights wash out the starlight. But out on the island, the sky gets real dark, and you can see billions and billions of stars. And I would just go stand outside with my telescope and look at them, for like, hours," Pam said.

"Wait," Matthew said, confused. "You stood outside? I thought you said you guys all floated, like me?"

Pamela pursed her lips, annoyed. "I was getting to that part," she said.

"Not all of us started floating at birth, you know."

"Oh. No, I didn't know that," said Matthew.

"How would he?" chimed in Liam. "He's only just found out there are other floaters a few minutes ago!"

"Well, now he's ruined my story," complained Pam.

"Oh, come off it," Pete grumbled, his eyes turned upward.

"I'm sorry," said Matthew. "Please, finish. I want to hear what happens."

Pam looked at him, then relented. "All right. I suppose I can conclude, even though the drama has been ruined."

Calvin chuckled. "We appreciate it, Pam."

"So anyway," Pam went on. "There I was, looking up at the stars, when all of a sudden, I felt this whoosh of air blowing against my face, and down my sides. Through the telescope, I saw an airplane passing by that suddenly seemed to be getting closer and closer. When I lowered the telescope, I realized I was flying through the air. A minute later, here I was. It was all over before I even really had a chance to know what was happening." She folded her arms and raised her eyebrow, apparently finished with her story.

"So...you never floated at all then, until the very moment you came here?" asked Matthew.

"Not that I know of," replied Pamela. "You can imagine my surprise when that went down, even though, technically, I was floating up."

"Fascinating," said Matthew. "And who was here when you got here?"

"Just Calvin," said Pamela.

Matthew looked at Calvin, who nodded, confirming this. "So you were all alone up here?" he asked.

"For awhile, yes," he replied. Calvin was easily the oldest, and he seemed to effortlessly fulfill the role of the small group's leader, exuding a demeanor of calm and wisdom.

"For how long? When did you get here?"

"As long as I can remember," said Calvin.

Matthew was confused. "You mean...you were born here?"

Calvin stroked his chin thoughtfully, leaning back into his cloud. "I don't think so," he replied. "I suppose I could have been...but in that case, I don't know where my parents went. More likely I was born down there, then floated up here as a baby."

"My goodness," said Matthew. "So you grew up here in the Sky?"

"Yup," said Calvin. "The Sky is all I've ever known, really. In fact, I had never seen or spoken to another person until Pam got here."

"Bet ya preferred it that way, she being yer first," quipped Pete.

"Shut up, brat!" shot back Pam, swatting at Pete's arm.

"Proving my point," said Pete dryly.

"That's terrible," said Matthew to Calvin. "You must have been so lonely."

"It wasn't really like that. I mean, it's not like I had anybody to miss. I looked down at the Earth the way you probably look at the moon – like a faraway land I was curious about, but never really yearned to go to. The Sky is my home, and always will be."

"But...no other people to talk to...I mean, you probably didn't even know how to speak English! Or any other language, for that matter."

"You're right. I didn't," Calvin smiled. "Fortunately, Pam talks a lot, so she made for a very good teacher."

"Why is everybody picking on me?" complained Pam, exasperated.

"Just kidding, Pammy," said Calvin, winking at her.

"That's amazing," said Matthew. "So you never even spoke until you were a teenager? How old are you now?"

"Not sure, exactly," said Calvin, furrowing his brow. "I never really thought to keep track."

"We estimate he's about 17," said Liam matter-of-factly. "But we could be off by one or two years in either direction."

"It's not that I didn't speak, exactly," Calvin said. "It's just that I didn't speak to another person."

"So...you talked to yourself? Like, out loud?" Matthew asked, confused.

"It's hard to explain," replied Calvin slowly. "I mean, I had thoughts, of course. And yes, I think I said things out loud, to myself, or the universe, or whatever...although I can't really remember what language those things were in...if it was a language at all." He shrugged his shoulders and smiled. "All I can tell you is, it made sense to me at the time."

"I see," said Matthew. He looked at Antonella, who was playing with the cloud, pulling it apart like wisps of cotton candy. "What about you, Antonella? Where are you from?"

"Argentina," she said without looking up.

"Argentina? I don't even know where that is," confessed Matthew.

"It's in South America," replied Antonella.

"Ahh...so you must speak Spanish, then?"

"*Sí.*"

Matthew chuckled. "And what's your story, Antonella?"

Still playing with the cloud, Antonella recited her background to Matthew, as if she had done it dozens of times before. "My mom and dad tied me to the bed all the time so I wouldn't float away. I always watched the birds outside my window when I was in bed, and I always wanted to fly like they could, since I knew I could do it. So I wriggled around until I wriggled out of my bed ties. Then when my mom and dad were gone, I opened the window and I flew away. And then I came here."

"You're a very brave little girl," said Matthew. "Don't you miss your home?"

"A little bit, but not really. Mom and Dad just made me stay in bed all the time, and I hated it. I love it up here. I can do whatever I want."

"Fair enough," said Matthew. He turned to the twins. "What about you guys?" he asked. "It must've been a bit better for you, having each other, right? Did you both start floating at the same time?"

Liam just kind of stared down at the cloud, as if he hadn't even heard Matthew. Similarly, Pete was inspecting his fingernails, and also didn't respond. Matthew started to speak again. "Guys? I said—"

"They don't like to talk about it," whispered Pam loudly to Matthew.

"They don't like to talk about what?" whispered back Matthew. "I was just curious if they started float—"

"We don't like to talk about it, mate," snapped Pete, glaring up at Matthew. "So let's move the conversation along, shall we?"

Matthew was taken aback. He hadn't meant any offense; indeed, the last thing he wanted to do was make a bad impression with this new group of floating peers he had found. "O-okay, sure. That's fine." He looked over at Calvin. "So that's it, huh? There's just six of us up here?"

"It would seem so," Calvin replied. "Although for a long time, it was just me. Then came Pam, and there were two. Then the twins, then Antonella, and now you. So one thing's for sure: we're growing. Slowly but surely."

"Why?" asked Matthew. "What are we meant to be doing up here?"

Calvin looked at him and smiled. "Your guess is as good as mine, Matthew."

5

By this time, it was growing rather dark out. The sky had become a beautiful shade of deep purple, and when Matthew looked up, he could see more stars than he ever had before in his life. The moon was only about a quarter full, but it shone brightly enough that he could still see the faces of the Nubivagants around him as they started to stand up and stretch.

"What do we do now?" Matthew asked.

"I'm knackered," said Liam. "I'm gonna hit the sack."

"I imagine you must be pretty exhausted yourself, with the day you've had," Calvin said to Matthew. He hadn't thought about it till just now, but Matthew *was* pretty tired.

Was it really only today his parents told him they'd talk after school, the same day he had been chased by Chad and his sidekicks? Suddenly, his eyelids felt very heavy. "Yeah, I guess I am," he replied.

"Come on," Calvin said, patting him on the back. "I'll help you make up a bed." He began walking Matthew away from the others, to a more secluded portion of the Sky.

"Goodnight Matthew!" the others called after him. "Welcome to the Sky! We're glad to have you!"

"Goodnight everybody," he said, waving. Suddenly, a nervousness began building inside of Matthew, as he started to realize he could not just go home to his mom and dad like he always did. For the first time, he wondered how – and if – he would ever see them again.

Calvin led him over to a nice, fluffy, billowy patch of cloud, and set about molding and shaping a big chunk of it into a very comfortable looking bed, just the right size for a little boy. As he worked, he looked up at Matthew, and could tell something was bothering him. "What's the matter, buddy?"

"Oh...nothing, really," said Matthew. "I was just..."

"You're wondering if you'll be able to go home."

"Yeah," said Matthew. "How'd you know?"

"Everyone's like that at the beginning," Calvin said, finishing up the bed. It didn't take him more than a minute or two. He even spun a hunk of cloud into a sort of blanket, which he laid atop the bed, then pulled it back for Matthew to get under. "It takes a little while to get over."

Matthew gingerly got into the cloud bed, surprised to find it supported his weight, and that it was, indeed, quite comfortable. The cloud seemed to mold to his body, like one of those fancy memory foam mattresses. He pulled the fluffy blanket up to his chin, and shivered a bit. "It's cold," he said.

"You'll get used to it, I promise," Calvin said. "The cloud actually does a pretty good job at keeping us warm. You'll see."

Matthew nodded. "So...then I won't be able to go home? Like, not ever?"

Calvin looked at him for a long moment, but didn't say anything. Off in the distance, up above them, bright lights streaked across the sky, then exploded brilliantly like fireworks, each one with a *pop!* sound. "Meteor shower," said Calvin, pointing at the fireworks. "Ever seen one before?"

"I've seen a shooting star," said Matthew. "But they never looked like that."

"A lot different up here, I reckon. You're a lot closer to the action." He turned back to Matthew, putting his hand comfortingly on his shoulder. "You're going to love it up here, Matthew. I promise. We all do." Matthew nodded, even though he was scared. Calvin added, "This is your home now."

"Okay," Matthew said, because he didn't know what else to say.

"Get some sleep. I'll see you in the morning." Calvin stood up, then walked off, fading into the darkness.

Matthew lay in his cloud bed, staring up at the brilliant meteor shower. Tears began filling his eyes. This was all so overwhelming. On the one hand, he was delighted and fascinated to learn there were other people like him, who he could relate to and who had similar experiences to his. He didn't feel so alone anymore. On the other hand, the thought of never seeing his parents again...of spending the rest of his life here in the clouds...he couldn't believe that was possible. Everything felt like a dream.

He could still hear the faint sounds of Pete and Pam talking as he lay there, his eyes closing. It reminded him of an overnight camping trip he had been on with his class the year before, when he had laid in his sleeping bag by himself with his boots on, listening to all the other children talk and laugh. He had felt so lonely then.

Maybe that will change now, Matthew thought to himself, as he drifted off to sleep. He was utterly exhausted. It had been the most eventful day of his life. *Maybe I won't be so lonely anymore.*

6

Matthew woke up early the next morning to behold the most brilliant sunrise he had ever seen. To be fair, he hadn't seen a great many sunrises, because like most little boys, he was usually asleep when they occurred. But of all the ones he had seen, this one definitely took the cake.

If you've never seen a sunrise from 30,000 feet up in the atmosphere before, I highly recommend it, as the experience is much more glorious than a sunrise viewed from Earth. Instead of watching the vivid oranges and purples and blues light up the sky from afar, as if you are staring at a painting being created off in the distance, in the Sky you feel like you are in the sunrise itself, as if you are a part of it. The colors appear to be exploding in slow motion all around you, until finally the sun takes its rightful place in the sky above you. It really is magnificent.

Before long the sun settled above Matthew, and it was blindingly bright. He had to squint just to be able to see. He put his hand against his forehead and looked around. Most of the others were up, milling about on the clouds.

Matthew got out of his bed, his bare feet sinking down into the surface of the cloud. This was still a very strange sensation for him: being able to move about normally, without the use of his gravity boots, and without floating up into the air. It felt weird, but also incredibly liberating – kind of like when you've had braces on your teeth for a couple years, then get them removed. Those first few hours of running your tongue over your teeth is a strangely divine feeling – almost as if they have just been released from prison.

Flexing his toes into the cool sponginess of the cloud, Matthew savored this sensation for a moment. Then he made his way over to some of the others. Calvin, Liam and Pam were sitting together, playing with Antonella and snacking on tufts of cloud. When they saw Matthew, they broke into smiles.

"Morning, mate!" Liam called out to him as he came over. "How was your first night in the Sky?"

"Pretty good," Matthew said as he sat down with them. "Pretty great actually, now that I think about it. I feel so...refreshed!" He did, too. He was just realizing he had probably slept better last night than he had in a long time.

"It's the air," Pam said. "You won't find air fresher than this down there." She pointed down, towards the edge of the cloud a few feet away.

Matthew looked off the edge, seeing the world below him for the first time. It was downright breathtaking. "Wow," he said, standing back up and walking towards the edge.

He could see for hundreds of miles below: vast stretches of land, dotted with pockets of civilization. He saw clusters of buildings, with highways leading in and out of them. He saw a lake, the blue water glistening in the sun, and around the lake were thousands of great green trees. And off in the distance, he could see a mountain range rising up into the sky...yet still far below where he was standing.

Matthew had been on an airplane a few times, when his parents had taken him on vacation – once to Los Angeles, to go to Disneyland, and also to visit his two sets of grandparents in Michigan and Texas. He remembered being fascinated looking out the window, marveling at how tiny everything was below him. He had that same feeling now, although it was greatly amplified by the fact that he was outside and felt like a part of it all – not just a spectator passing through in a flying aluminum capsule.

Just then, as Matthew was taking in the view, little Antonella sprinted right past him – and jumped off the cloud! "NO!!!" Matthew screamed out, reaching for her – but it was too late! She went sailing past him, falling

down below...before settling to a stop a good ten feet or so below him. Then, just like that, she popped back up, drawn towards the cloud like a magnet. Giggling, she climbed back onto the cloud next to Matthew and looked up at him, delighted.

"Gotcha!" she squealed, laughing, before running back to the others, who were chuckling as well.

"Good one, kid," said Calvin, dragging her by the ankles toward him and ruffling her hair. "She's a little trickster," he explained to Matthew.

Matthew was too stunned to speak, or even breathe. He realized his hand was over his heart, squeezing the flesh on his chest. Only after a moment did he feel it resume beating again.

"S'okay," said Liam. "No danger of falling up here."

"Think about it," Pam said. "If you could fall down, you wouldn't be up here in the first place."

"Go ahead. Give it a try!" urged Calvin.

Matthew turned and looked back over the edge, terrified. "You mean...I can just..." He looked back at them, unable to verbalize what Antonella had just done.

"Of course! It's perfectly safe. Believe me, if you could get off this cloud, one of us would have done it by now. Not that we don't love it up here," Liam confessed. "Although I wouldn't mind a thick, juicy burger once in awhile."

"Again with these burgers," said Calvin curiously. "The way you talk about them, it really makes me wonder what I'm missing."

"You have no idea," groaned Liam longingly.

Matthew peered down over the edge again, the Earth drifting quietly by beneath him. "Okay," he breathed to himself. "Here goes nothing..." Gingerly, he picked one foot up, held it out over the empty sky...and fell forward.

A little involuntary yelp escaped his mouth as he pitched off the edge of the cloud, and for a moment he was perhaps even more terrified than watching Antonella fake-plummet to her death. But then, after falling just a few feet, he too stabilized, hovering for a second in thin air, before rising right back up. It was as if he was in a swimming pool, and the cloud was the edge surrounding it.

He placed his hands on the lip of the cloud, peering back at the others, who pointed at him, laughing with delight. "See?" said Pam happily. "That proves it. You're one of us!"

A huge grin broke out on Matthew's face. *I think I'm gonna like it here,* he thought to himself. Then he took a big bite out of the cloud in front of his face, gulping down the refreshing goodness.

7

Moments later, Matthew was having an absolute ball playing with little Antonella, running all around the clouds. She showed him how you could dive down through the clouds, then come popping back up, just as if they were walking on water – which, of course, they were.

The others joined in, including Pete (who liked to sleep late, it turns out), and before long the six of them were chasing each other around, sprinting and diving head first across the clouds. Arms extended like wings, Matthew discovered he could skid dozens of feet at a time, sending showers of mist up into the air. Then he and the others took turns picking up Antonella and tossing her across the Sky as she shrieked in delight, her little body causing the great big poofs of cloud banks to explode in plumes of white.

"Let's go climbing!" Pete suggested, once they had had their fill of that game. He pointed at a huge, billowing cloud formation that rose up into the heavens like a puffy white mountain.

"You boys go ahead," said Pam, embracing Antonella like a stuffed animal. "We're gonna stay here and snuggle."

"Suit yourself," said Calvin. "Come on, boys!" He and Pete dashed across the Sky towards the cloud mountain, with Liam and Matthew running after them.

They reached the base of the humongous formation, then began climbing, digging their feet into the sides of it. Matthew grabbed the cloud and pulled himself upwards, and soon was scrabbling up the sides of the cloud mountain with ease, close behind the others. It was much easier and more fun than climbing a regular mountain, as each time he pushed off with his feet, the cloud seemed to spring him upwards like a trampoline, so that he was bouncing his way higher and higher.

After a while, the four boys reached the summit of the mountain. They stopped to enjoy the view, looking out over the Earth for hundreds of miles. They could see a giant brown desert going on forever, and running right through the middle of it was what looked like an enormous, jagged crack. "I reckon that's the Grand Canyon," said Liam.

"Whoa," Matthew said, blown away. He had only seen images of the Grand Canyon on TV, or in magazines. He couldn't believe he was now looking down at the real thing, from thousands of feet up. It was so beautiful and magnificent, it didn't even look real. It looked more like a painting, gliding silently beneath them.

"Hey boys!" they heard a faint call coming from down below. They turned and looked, seeing the tiny shapes of Pam and Antonella waving at them from back down at the base of the cloud mountain.

"Heya!" Pete waved his arms back at the girls. "Look out below!" He turned and grinned at the others. "Last one down's a great gob o' goo." With that, Pete dove forward, sliding back down the mountain.

Matthew watched him, stunned at how Pete could just fling himself down the giant cloud like that. But before he could react, Calvin grabbed him around the waist and hoisted him into the air. "Come on, Matty. Off you go!" And he tossed him forward, right off the side of the mountain, sending him careening downward!

Matthew screamed with delight as he tumbled through the clouds, bouncing every which way. Out of the corner of his eye he caught glimpses of the other boys skidding uncontrollably, flipping head over heels, shrieking with laughter, until they all reached the bottom, sliding to a stop. Matthew's heart was pounding so hard, and he found himself unable to contain his giggling. Never had he felt so exhilarated!

Minutes later, after everyone had calmed down, Matthew was sitting back in a circle with everyone, just relaxing and talking. The conversation flowed from one subject to another effortlessly, and he surprised himself simply by participating. He felt quite at ease talking about anything and everything, including himself. In fact, he couldn't remember ever having talked so much, or so easily, in his entire life! The mere experience of simply hanging out with other kids was so new to him, and so enjoyable, he couldn't get over how purely good he felt.

And the others noticed. "Matty," said Calvin at one point. "I don't think I've seen you stop smiling all day."

No one had ever called him "Matty" before. It felt good having a nickname – like he finally had good enough friends to qualify for one. He smiled even wider, shrugging his shoulders. "I guess I'm just enjoying myself," Matthew said.

"Told you," said Calvin, winking at him. Before he knew it, the sun was setting again. It was absolutely gorgeous, lighting the sky up in brilliant red and pink and purple hues. They all watched as it settled down beneath the Earth's horizon, far below them. Matthew looked up, as once again the sky began filling up with billions of bright white stars.

"What happened to the day?" he asked with puzzled wonderment. Pete and Liam both laughed in unison.

"What d'you mean?" asked Liam.

"It went by so fast," Matthew said. "I feel like I just woke up, and now all of a sudden it's nighttime again!"

"That's how time works," said Pete sarcastically.

"Don't listen to him," said Pam. "Up here, the days have a way of flying by..."

"Which is the precise effect that having fun has on time," smiled Liam. "It's science."

Matthew gazed back out over the land below him, as the lights of a city in the desert began twinkling. It was amazing, he thought to himself. It felt like he'd barely been awake a couple hours. How was that possible? But

Matthew *had* had fun today. In fact, it was the most fun he'd ever had in his whole life. Only now, as he thought about going to sleep again, did his thoughts turn back to his parents for the first time all day.

But the sadness he felt the previous night was not quite as painful. It stung a little bit less. He had no idea what was in store for him up here, or if he'd ever see his mom and dad again. But now he had a budding feeling that everything was starting to turn towards the good, instead of that exhausting, negative dread he was so used to. He felt like a person who had been sick for years, but was now finally starting to heal.

After he said goodnight to the others, as he shaped a heap of cloud into a circular little nest to sleep in, then climbed in and got comfortable, he spoke softly under his breath. "I love you, Mommy. I love you, Dad," he whispered into the darkness. He had more he wanted to say, in hopes the universe could somehow carry his message to his parents. But before he had a chance to get it out, he had fallen fast asleep.

8

"Now that you're one of us, you've got to dress like us," said Pete to Matthew the next morning.

Matthew looked at the others, all wearing their cloud clothes in some fashion or another. "All right," he said, a little hesitant. "But...I don't know how to make them like you do."

"I'll show you," said Pam. "I'm an amazing designer." She walked over to Matthew, sizing him up, taking measurements with her hands. Then, she bent down, grabbed a whole armful of cloud, and began packing, shaping and spinning it into a tightly woven garment.

To Matthew's amazement, within just a few minutes she was finished, holding up an elegant, shimmering white robe, almost befitting of royalty. "How does that look?" she asked.

"It looks amazing," said Matthew, impressed.

Pam beamed. "Go ahead. Try it on."

Matthew blanched, shy. "What...right now?"

"Oh come on, mate," said Pete, slapping him on the back. "We're family now."

"Don't worry, we'll turn around," said Pamela. "Come on, guys, give him some privacy."

Everyone turned their backs to Matthew. After a moment of talking himself into it, he quickly got undressed, putting on the robe.

"Okay," he said. "You can turn back around now."

They did. "Wow," said Calvin. "Looking sharp, buddy!"

"Indeed," confirmed Liam, feeling the robe. "You'll have to make me one of these, Pam."

"What do you think?" Pam asked Matthew.

"I love it," Matthew replied, holding his arms out, admiring his new cloud robe. He did, too. He found it to be infinitely more comfortable than anything else he had ever worn. Talk about breathable fabric! It was as if he was wearing the coolest, softest pajamas ever created. "What should I do with my old clothes?" he asked.

"Toss 'em," said Pete. "Won't be needing those anymore. That life's behind you now."

"You mean...just...?"

"Just drop 'em, mate," Pete said, a serious tone in his voice. "Open yer hand and let 'em fall."

Matthew looked at the shirt, pants, underwear and socks in his hand. Then, he slowly let them slip out. They fell down through the cloud at his feet, and disappeared.

"Congratulations, mate," said Pete. "Yer officially a Nubivagant now." He held out his hand. Matthew looked at it...and smiled, shaking it. Then, Pete did something unexpected: he pulled Matthew in and hugged him.

"Thank you," said Matthew, touched. He had never officially been anything, other than an oddity, a weirdo. It felt incredible to be a part of this very exclusive group of kids – the Nubivagants – who accepted him for who he was. And now, one by one, they took turns hugging him, making him feel right at home.

9

Later on that day, the Nubivagants were sitting around, enjoying the sunshine and talking. They had just gotten done with an epic cloudball fight, in which they had divided up into teams of two, and engaged in battle by hurling balled up chunks of cloud at each other. It was exactly like a snowball fight – which, growing up in California, Matthew had never experienced – except when a cloudball strikes you, it bursts into a spray of poofy mist, and isn't nearly as cold as snow. Everyone agreed Matthew was a natural, having knocked Pete right off his feet with a well-thrown cloudball directly to the face. Pete had not been as amused as everyone else.

Now, during their downtime, as Liam and Pete were telling a story about their one-eyed Irish uncle (whose name was, appropriately, One-Eyed Wally), the Nubivagants suddenly heard a loud rumbling. It sounded like it was coming from far away, but it quickly got louder, indicating it was coming closer.

"Airplane!" Antonella cried out, excited. And with that warning cry, the others sprang into action.

"Move, move, move!!!" yelled Calvin, taking charge. He led everyone across the cloud, quick as they could run, until they reached a big, puffy white cloud bank. The Nubivagants all hid behind it as the sound of the approaching rumble grew to become deafening.

Matthew peeked over the edge of the cloud, just as an enormous white jumbo jetliner appeared, churning up the clouds as it flew past. He stared, agape, as he watched it go by. Matthew had always been under the impression that airplanes fly very fast – which they must, I suppose, to be able to get across the country in a matter of hours. But have you ever been in a plane and looked out the window? Everything seems to be passing by

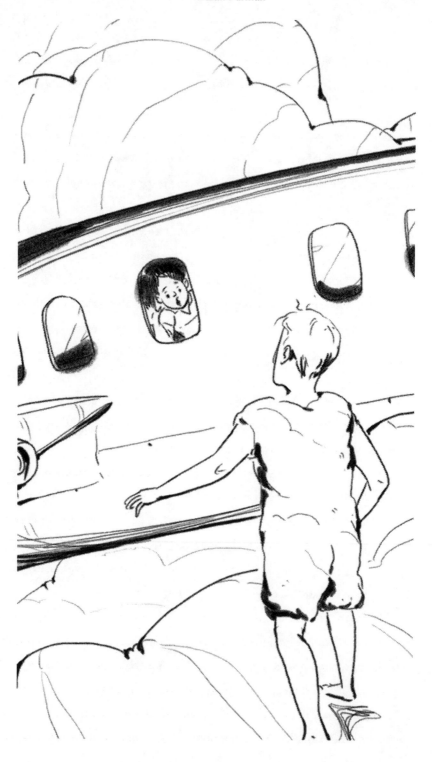

at just sort of a regular speed, doesn't it? Not some blurry super-high speed, as if the world outside was stuck on fast-forward. And that phenomenon goes both ways. Looking at the plane from the outside, it too appears to be passing by at regular speed.

Matthew could actually see the people in the airplane, through the windows, as it went by. There they were, not ten feet away from him, reading or sleeping or watching movies on the little screens in the backs of the chairs in front of them.

And then, one little boy who wasn't much younger than Matthew himself, turned and looked out his window. In fact...he looked right at Matthew.

For a brief instant, Matthew and the boy on the plane made eye contact. The boy definitely saw him, because his eyes went wide, and his mouth fell open, amazed. Then he turned to his mother, who was sleeping soundly beside him, and shook her arm to wake her up and look at the boy who was outside the window, hiding behind a cloud.

Groggy, the little boy's mother looked out the window, but saw nothing other than regular old clouds, without any people on them, and, a bit annoyed, scolded her son and went back to sleep. The reason she did not see anything out of the ordinary is because right as she had turned to look, Pete had grabbed Matthew by the collar of his robe, and yanked him back through the cloud, out of sight of the plane's passengers.

"Don't ever let them see you!" he yelled sternly, standing over Matthew.

Matthew looked up at Pete, frightened. He could see he was angry. "Easy, Pete," said Calvin, gently placing his hand on his chest, backing him away a step. Then he extended his hand, helping Matthew up. "Sorry about that, Matty. I should have told you. We don't want anyone to know about us, about us being up here. It doesn't happen too often, but if ever there's a chance someone might see us, we do whatever we can to prevent that from happening."

"But why?" asked Matthew, confused.

"They'll be bad to us," said Antonella simply.

"Nothing good will come of it, that's why not," said Pete. "People didn't treat ya very well down there when they thought ya were different, did they?" Matthew shook his head no. "Yeah, so imagine what they'd do if they knew we were up here," Pete continued. "They'd come up in helicopters, throw a big fishing net over us, and take us right back down to the ground. They'd lock us up in some laboratory, stick us with needles, and treat us like absolute freaks."

"And you guys say *I'm* dramatic," said Pam, rolling her eyes.

"I don't care!" screamed Pete, upset. "I'm not going back down there." He turned to Matthew, poking his finger into his chest. "If ya want to be one of us, ya can't ever make contact with the people on the ground again. Understand?"

Matthew looked around. The others didn't seem to be quite as passionate about this issue as Pete was, but they weren't disputing it, either. "I'm afraid it's true, Matthew," said Calvin. "That's our policy. I don't have any real knowledge of the ground, but from what the others tell me, they're not very accepting of people like us. And it sounds like that was your experience as well."

Matthew thought about this, and had to nod in agreement. "I guess you're right," he said.

"All right," said Calvin. "Well, like I said – most of the time you shouldn't have to worry about it, as there isn't much opportunity to interact with them."

"But just so we're on the same page," pressed Pete, sternly. "If ever there *is* an opportunity...you attempt no contact. Agreed?" He held out his hand for Matthew to shake.

Matthew looked at the others, then back at Pete. He nodded again.

"Agreed," he said, shaking his hand.

"Great," said Calvin, just as he noticed a blustery wind picking up, swirling the clouds around their feet. "Ah," he smiled at the others. "Who's up for a game of Bumper Clouds?"

10

What followed was Matthew's introduction to the wild and wonderful weather patterns of the Sky. You see, the clouds were always moving around the Earth. Most of the time, they were just lazily gliding along, so slowly they were seemingly at rest. But when the wind started blowing, as it was now, they began zipping through the atmosphere at such high speeds it blew the Nubivagants' hair backwards, as if they were riding in a convertible.

During such bursts of gustiness, the group had the chance to play their favorite game: Bumper Clouds. Each kid stood on his or her own chunk of cloud, positioning themselves with their feet balanced on it like a skateboard. Then, through some shuffling and jiggering, they were able to actually break their own chunk – their Bumper Cloud car – away from the rest of the surface.

And then, with the wind at their backs – away they went! Each Nubivagant had the ability, with a little practice, to control how their clouds moved. They could actually steer them with the weight and balance of their bodies, riding the wind like a surfer rides the waves.

After some coaching from Calvin, Matthew got himself set up on his own bumper cloud. "Ready?" Calvin asked him, the wind beginning to swirl heavily around them, pushing their clouds forward.

Matthew wobbled a bit, unsteady on his feet. "Do I have a choice?" he asked nervously.

"Nope!" shouted Pete above the howling wind. "Good luck, rookie!" With expert balance, Pete crouched down, shifting his weight forward. Matthew watched as his cloud took off across the sky ahead of him.

"Whoa," Matthew said to himself, as Liam zoomed past him as well.

He was still wobbling, his cloud jerking up and down in the wind shakily.

"You'll get the hang of it, Matty," said Calvin. "Just keep riding till the wind dies down. Oh, and I almost forgot...don't let the others knock you down!"

"Knock me down?" asked Matthew. "Why would they knock me down?"

"Why do you think it's called Bumper Clouds?" Calvin hollered, grinning, before catching a wind gust, taking off after the twins.

Confused, Matthew turned to his right to see Pam driving her cloud straight toward him, with Antonella riding on her back! He ducked just in time to avoid her smashing into him. She zipped over his head, and looked back, cackling. "Nice reflexes!" she shouted.

"Yeah, nice reflexes!" repeated Antonella, as the two girls laughed and sped off.

Matthew gritted his teeth, determined now to compete. "All right," he muttered under his breath to himself. "I got this." With a bit more confidence, he took control of his cloud, planting his feet firmly into the surface, and leaning forward. To his delight, the cloud caught a nice updraft of wind, and lurched forward. In an instant, he was flying across the sky, arms outstretched like an eagle's wings, the wind crashing against his face and screaming in his ears.

"*WHOOOOOOOOOOOOO!!!!!!!*" Matthew shrieked, exhilarated. He could see the others come back into focus ahead of him, as he rocketed closer towards them. Within seconds, he had caught up to them, zipping and zooming right alongside them.

Pete looked over, surprised to see him. "Oy!" he shouted. "Looks like ya got some skills, mate!"

"I guess so!" Matthew shouted back.

"Let's see how ya do with a little turbulence!" Pete grinned wickedly, steering his cloud into Matthew's, bumping him and throwing him off balance.

"Hey!" Matthew said, grinning back. He managed to regain his balance, right in time to see Liam coming at him from the other direction. His eyes nearly popped out of their sockets, as he braced for the impact. But then, his instincts took over. He leaned back hard, sending his cloud jumping up ten feet in the air, like a jet fighter pilot pulling out of a free fall. Looking below, he watched as Liam missed him entirely, and crashed into his own brother! The two of them screamed as their cloud cars burst apart in gigantic explosions of mist, sending each brother careening off into the air. But of course, there was no danger of falling back to Earth...after flying for a few seconds through the air, the magical pull of the clouds brought them safely back to the Sky.

However, they had lost the game – an outcome Pete was not particularly pleased with, and he let Liam know about it. "What'd ya do that for?" he whined. "I was about to tip him!"

"I had a clear shot!" Liam defended himself. "How was I supposed to know he was gonna pull up like that? That's an advanced move!"

"You ruined us both! Next time mind yer own business!"

"Ah, you're just mad you lost to a newbie."

Matthew could hear the two brothers' squabbling fade away as he continued on, but the game was still going. He had to stay focused. "Watch out, kid!" shouted Calvin as he crisscrossed right in front of Matthew, barely missing him. Matthew gasped, watching as Calvin curbed his cloud against the wind like a jet ski against the waves, then came back towards him. He turned to see Pam and Antonella directly in front of him, just a few feet away. Yelping in fright, he crouched and leaned hard against the front of his cloud, sending it nose-diving straight down, narrowly avoiding a collision.

This race went on for about a half hour, as Matthew, Calvin and the girls pursued each other. The Pam-Antonella team met their end when they turned too sharply into a giant cloudbank, disappearing into the white mountain, their cloud car destroyed, but giggling maniacally the whole time.

In the end, Matthew and Calvin found themselves next to each other, the wind howling in their ears as they sized each other up. They went back and forth, bumping their clouds up against each other, each trying to throw the other off course. But just as they reached peak speed, Matthew looked over into Calvin's eyes, and gave him a confident smile. Before Calvin could react, Matthew jerked his cloud hard to the right, catching the back edge of Calvin's cloud, spinning it in circles at a dizzying speed. Unable to hold on, Calvin tumbled off his vapor vessel and fell through the air, landing in a poof of grey as his cloud car came apart in all directions.

Matthew looked back, laughing. He had won his first game of Bumper Clouds – the first of many to come.

As the wind died down, Matthew steered his cloud – the only one still intact – drifting back towards the others, who were waiting for him in the Sky.

"Not bad," said Pete, smoothing out his disheveled black hair, "for a rookie."

Matthew shrugged as his cloud was reabsorbed by the larger white surface of the Sky, an enormously smug grin plastered across his face. "Beginner's luck," he said, then grabbed a hunk of cloud and stuffed it in his mouth.

11

Later that afternoon, after the wind subsided, Matthew noticed the clouds beneath his feet had become exceedingly soggy. He found it much more difficult to walk around; he had to slog through them to get around, his feet sinking deep into the heavy, squishy surface, as if he was wading around in piles of wet towels.

"It's raining!" cried Antonella joyfully. She jumped up, tucked her knees into her chest and cannonballed down through the clouds, causing a massive splash as she fell through the bottom, then popped back up completely soaked, laughing hysterically. It wasn't long before the others joined in, taking turns jumping and diving down through the clouds and into the rain.

Because it was still daytime, and the sun was still above the clouds, they dried right off within a few moments. It was quite a bizarre and exhilarating experience to go from playing in the bright, warm, shining sunlight to diving under the cloud and immediately being in the middle of a rainstorm – only to go right back to basking in the sunlight again an instant later. Matthew couldn't get enough of it.

Then, it started to *really* rain hard – which was an event Matthew would never forget.

According to Liam, they were somewhere over Southeast Asia – Cambodia maybe, or Vietnam – and the clouds they were sitting on began raining very heavily, as they often do in that part of the world. "Here we go!" he exclaimed happily. "I think we're about to get some action!"

"Yes!" said Pam, as she and Pete hi-fived and sprang to their feet. "Man, it's been awhile," said Calvin.

"Awhile since what? What kind of action?" asked Matthew, standing up with the others, as they followed Liam hurriedly towards the center of the cloud they were hanging out on.

"Oh, this is your first one! How exciting!" said Liam.

"I remember my first one," breathed Pam excitedly. "I just about peed my cloud-pants."

"You're in for a show," said Calvin. "Come on!"

Everyone ran over to a spot in the cloud that seemed to be glowing. They stood in a circle, looking down, as a spectacular sight developed right under their feet.

Swirls of blue and white electricity were circling around in the cloud in chaotic patterns, little sparks shooting off every couple seconds in all directions. Matthew stared as the swirls began gathering speed, racing around faster and faster. The cloud began to glow even more brightly.

"Here it comes!" cried Liam.

Matthew looked up at the others, excited and scared. Pete smirked at him mischievously. "Cover yer ears, mate," he offered, putting his hands over his own ears. Matthew followed his lead, as did everyone else, as he stepped an inch or two closer to the swirling circle of blue light by his feet.

And then, when the swirling electricity reached a furious fever pitch, producing a high-pitched humming noise – *BOOM!!!* There was an astoundingly loud clap of thunder, so loud it shocked Matthew to his bones, even with his hands over his ears. But what happened beneath him was truly a magnificent sight.

At the same time the sound of the thunder exploded in his ears, a bolt of lightning shot out of the cloud, streaking down across the sky to the Earth below. When this happened, it created a hole in the cloud about five feet wide, so Matthew could watch as the lightning zigged and zagged downwards before halting for just a split second, then disappeared altogether, vanishing into thin air. A second later, the cloud reformed around the hole the lightning came from, leaving no trace of anything unusual.

"WOW!!!" Matthew shouted. It was easily the most incredible thing he had ever seen. Only a few days ago, he was mystified by the sunrise, but that was no comparison to this event. He looked up at the others, his mind blown. "Did you see that? That was amazing! That was awesome! That was —"

"Uh, Matthew?" Pam interrupted.

"Yes?"

"I think you might have gotten a little too close to the lightning," she said, eyes down, suppressing a giggle. Matthew looked down, horrified to see he was stark naked. The sheer power of the lighting bolt had created a vacuum, so that anything near it was instantly sucked down through the hole in the cloud. In Matthew's unfortunate case, that happened to be his cloud robe.

"EWWW!!!" Antonella screamed with shock and laughter, as a mortified Matthew covered himself as quick as he could, collapsing to the cloud and folding over, trying to make himself as small as possible. If he could have disappeared, he would have.

"Hard to say who's put on the better show – you or the storm," joked Pete.

"Don't look at me!" Matthew wailed. "Pam! Pam, can you make me a new robe? Like right now please???"

Pam obliged Matthew, mostly because everyone wanted to get back to watching the lightning storm – which wasn't over, not by a long shot. If you've ever witnessed such a storm, you know lightning doesn't just happen once. No, a really good storm can produce dozens of lightning bolts across the sky – hundreds even! And it just so happened this was a really good storm.

Indeed, for hours (after Matthew was dressed in his new cloud-fit), he and the others ran around to different areas of the Sky, wherever they noticed the churning circles of light brewing beneath the cloud's surface. Even after it got dark, and the others got tired and eventually went one by one off to bed, Matthew stayed up, fascinated, watching every lightning bolt he could find.

Like gigantic electrified snowflakes, no two lightning bolts were quite the same. Each one streaked across the sky in a different pattern. Some lasted longer than others, reaching further down towards the Earth. In fact, the most brilliant bolt Matthew saw traveled all the way to the ground, making contact with a tree. He watched from up high as the tree exploded with magnificent bright white sparks, then burned brightly with fire for a few moments before the rain eventually put it out.

Matthew had never seen special effects so spectacular in all the movies he had ever seen! He couldn't believe nature could provide this sort of entertainment. Watching the lightning instantly became his favorite pastime, and every time it rained after that storm, he got very excited, hoping for another round of lightning.

And yet, he had absolutely no idea how important this phenomenon would figure into his own destiny, just a few months from now.

12

When he wasn't having the time of his life playing endless fun-filled invented games, or sitting around chatting with the other Nubivagants about anything and everything they could think of, Matthew discovered one of his favorite pastimes to be simply sitting at the edge of the Sky, looking down on various parts of the vast world below him.

Sometimes it was a lush, green jungle. The next day it was a huge mountain range, the peaks covered in bright white snow, reaching high into the sky, not too far below the cloud Matthew sat upon. Sometimes he spent day after day passing over an enormous brown, dry desert, with nary an indication of life in sight. And sometimes weeks would be spent over the ocean, where Matthew might occasionally spot a little island or an ocean liner. These were rare and exciting observations, he realized, because the oceans are so vast, often there would be nothing but water for days. Never before had he comprehended quite how big and empty the sea was when he had seen it on a map in school. But nothing gives you perspective like floating around above the Earth on a cloud.

It was during one of these little sits on the Sky's edge that Matthew saw what looked to be an island, surrounded on both sides by rivers flowing out to an ocean. But the island wasn't like any Matthew had ever seen before – this one was jam-packed from end to end with buildings and enormous skyscrapers, with a huge green park right smack in the middle of it, and streets perfectly crisscrossing the length and the width of the island, like a grid. He stared down at this interesting, busy looking city with great fascination, when Pam came over and sat down next to him.

"That's New York City," she said.

"Really?" asked Matthew, intrigued. He had heard a great deal about

New York City, of course, and had seen it many times on TV and in movies. He grew up on the other side of the continent, where New York seemed as far away from him as the cloud he was sitting on now. Looking down on just how spectacular and enormous it was, it was yet another exciting moment in this completely surreal journey he was on.

"Yup," she said, getting a little teary-eyed. "It's the greatest city in the world. I miss it so much, it makes me cry every time we pass by it." She wiped her eyes, then pointed down. "I used to live there, to the right of Central Park, on Amsterdam Avenue." She held out her hand, which contained a skinny silver tube. "Here," she said. "Try using this. You can really see so much more."

Matthew looked at the tube. "Your telescope?" he asked.

"It's my most prized possession. My only possession," said Pam, raising her eyebrow at him. "So don't you dare drop it."

"Are you sure?" Matthew asked, apprehensive about being entrusted with such a valuable item.

"Of course," Pam said. "After all, you really *have* to see New York."

Matthew took the telescope from her hand, holding it carefully. He had used a telescope before, on a field trip to the planetarium, but that one was much bigger, and was affixed securely to a tripod. He had never seen one so small.

"Just look through here," Pam said, tapping the skinnier end of the telescope. "Use this dial to adjust the focus," she explained as she put it to her own eye and gazed out for a second. With an exaggerated sigh, she handed the scope over to Matthew. "It gets more beautiful every time."

Matthew looked through the lens, pointing the telescope down at the metropolis below. Everything looked very blurry, so he moved the little dial around, just like Pam had shown him. After a couple moments, he got the hang of it, and things began coming into focus.

Pow! All of a sudden, Matthew felt like he was right down there, in the middle of the busiest place he had ever seen! Enormous, magnificent buildings, cars and taxis and buses zipping through the streets...and people! So many people walking in every direction. They were tiny, but there they were, moving around on the streets like little bugs! Even from miles above the ground, he was confident he had never seen any place like this before.

Matthew looked up at Pam, ecstatic. "This is incredible!" he exclaimed. "I can see everything!"

Pam laughed. "I know," she said. "Isn't it great? It was my father's. He's an astronomer, and he made it himself. Thank god I was holding it when I came up here." She began to point at various landmarks throughout the city. "That's the Empire State Building...there's Rockefeller Center...and there out in the water, that's the Statue of Liberty."

"The Statue of Liberty," Matthew said to himself, gazing down at the majestic, tall green woman with the crown and torch, rising up out of the sea. How incredible it was, to be seeing such a famous site, from a view no one on Earth had ever held. In that moment, he felt like the luckiest boy alive. Even at eleven years old, he understood how important this experience was to someone who had never really traveled outside of his small town.

He stared down for another moment or two, as the glorious city slowly faded from view, and the Sky drifted out over the Atlantic Ocean. Then he looked up at Pam. "Thank you," he said, truly grateful. "Do you mind if I borrow this once in awhile?"

Pam laughed. "Sure, anytime you like." She hugged him lovingly. "In fact, hang onto it for a bit for me. I'm going to sunbathe." She ruffled Matthew's hair, got up and strode off across the cloud.

Matthew eagerly turned back to the view below, his eye pressed up against the eyepiece lens of the telescope. It wouldn't be long before he had a somewhat permanent ring around his eye from gazing through that telescope day after day, sometimes for hours at a time.

13

And so the days began to fly by, blurring one into the next, the way time does when you are enjoying life. Down on the ground, we sometimes find it challenging to keep track of the minutes, and occasionally hours. Up in the Sky, it was difficult to keep track of the days, months, even years. It was useless paying attention to seasons, because there were none. Seasons, in large part, differ by the type of weather they bring. Up here, the Nubivagants were a part of the weather bringing the seasons to those people down below. But their own environment was more or less unchanging, with the sun and moon endlessly taking turns above them. Even on the colder nights or scorching afternoons, the Nubivagants adapted to the weather around them rather easily, layering themselves in thicker or thinner cloud clothes.

Matthew felt so at home in the Sky, such a part of this small but wonderful group of people, in a way he had never experienced down on the ground. Everything was easy up here; every day brought some new, exciting experience. And best of all, there was no struggle. All the frustration, anxiety and negativity he routinely dealt with down on Earth seemed to simply not exist in the Sky.

Sometimes, when he felt like being by himself for a bit, he would wander off to another part of the cloud. He would walk for hours, across a cloudbank that stretched on for miles and miles. Matthew found these walks to be so peaceful, he truly did feel like he was in his own private heaven.

It was on one of these heavenly strolls when Matthew went up to a giant puff of clouds a bit larger than himself and, without even really realizing what he was doing, started sculpting the moist fluff into a sculpture. Hours went by in a blink, and by the time he finished, he had sculpted what looked to be a boy about his age. It was a bit crude, but no matter – Matthew had discovered a newfound passion.

Every day after that, Matthew took some time to create cloud sculptures. With a little practice he began getting better, and could soon form tigers and deer and cacti and little houses and whatever else his mind dreamed up. Each of the other kids modeled for him again and again, in a variety of poses, then delighted in seeing their likenesses recreated. Sometimes Matthew spent hours creating an entire village of cloud sculptures, only to realize he couldn't see what he was creating anymore, because the sun had gone down and it was already time for bed again. So he would go to sleep, then wake up in the morning to discover his sculptures had melted, their forms having disappeared back into the surface from which they came. Nothing was of any permanence in the Sky. But that didn't bother Matthew one bit. He simply set about on a whole new endeavor the next day.

There came a point where Matthew had no idea how long he had been in the Sky. It could have been a couple months; it could have been a couple years.

Indeed, he found it was getting more and more difficult to recall the time before he had arrived, the memories of his previous life growing fuzzier, like a dream that fades after you've woken up. It was at this point, sitting on the edge of the Sky, watching another magical sunset with his new family while slowly riding a warm air current over some tropical islands, that Matthew realized how purely happy he had become.

14

One afternoon not longer after, the clouds happened to be drifting imperceptibly slowly, practically sitting still, creating a very mellow, relaxing mood. The Nubivagants were lounging in pleasant silence, enjoying the atmosphere and a crisp chilliness that was nicely balanced by the warm sunshine.

Matthew was lazily sculpting a house – one that looked remarkably similar to the one he used to live in, only miniaturized – when he found his thoughts wandering back to his old life. "Do you guys ever miss it?" he asked the group suddenly.

"Miss what?" asked Antonella, who was balling up little wisps of cloud and blowing them away, like dandelion florets.

"Do you ever miss being back down there?"

"No," Pete said matter-of-factly. There was an uncomfortable beat of silence, which Calvin attempted to fill.

"We were not meant to exist down there," he said. "I can't speak for everyone, but I couldn't ask for a better life than what I have up here, especially now that I have all of you."

"But you never lived down there," said Matthew. "So there's nothing for you to really miss."

"I'd never return, even if I could walk normally," said Pete spitefully. "There's nothin' on Earth for us. We don't belong there, and I have no desire to go back."

"I miss my family," admitted Pam wistfully. "I miss talking with my sister, and my parents, the four of us just having dinner, or watching TV. And just the fact that they don't know what happened to me, you know...what they must think..." Pam stopped, choking up a bit. She wiped a tear from each eye. "That still hurts. It stings. I try not to think about it, and most of the time I don't. But that pain never goes away completely." She took a deep breath and tried to smile. "But I've been here long enough to accept that this is my home now. This is my family too. The Sky is where I belong, where each of us belongs...including you, Matthew."

Matthew thought about this. He did feel like he belonged in the Sky. He felt relaxed and carefree and, most importantly, he felt normal. In such a short amount of time, he considered the Nubivagants to be almost as much a family as the one he had on Earth.

And yet, until now he hadn't fully considered what his parents might have thought had happened to him. The idea that they were out looking for him, calling the police, worrying themselves sick...that was a particularly unpleasant thought. He didn't like to think about that at all.

"Have you ever...?" Matthew trailed off, not quite knowing what he wanted to ask next.

"Have we ever what?" asked Pam.

"I don't know, have you ever, like...tried to get back down, somehow? Or at least get a message to someone? Like, tell your family you're okay?"

The others looked at each other knowingly. Clearly, this was something they had also discussed extensively, with no resolution. It was left to little Antonella to ask the obvious question: "How?"

"We're stuck up here, mate," said Pete. "Like it or not, there's no getting back down."

Suddenly, a tree appeared right in the middle of the cloud they were sitting on! It seemed impossible, but there it was, the pointy needles of an evergreen poking up out of the grey mist, not ten feet away from them. "Look!" Matthew shouted, pointing at it.

"Holy cripes!" Pam said. "We're in a mountain cloud!"

"We haven't touched down in I don't know how long," remarked Calvin, his eyes dancing. "A year or two, maybe."

"What do you mean, touched down?" Matthew asked. "How is this possible?"

"Our altitude changes," explained Calvin. "You must have noticed sometimes we're higher up than other times."

Calvin was right – now that Matthew thought about it, the Earth did seem closer or further away on any given day, although he never paid it much mind. To Matthew's amazement, more of the mountainous surface was coming into view from their cloud, breaking up the white mist into little pockets here and there. A moment later, his bottom brushed against something solid. He looked down...and was shocked to see a giant rock beneath him!

"I'm on the ground!" he said, standing.

Calvin smiled knowingly. "Technically, you're still in the Sky," he said. "But enjoy this moment. It isn't often our two worlds converge like this."

Matthew stood up, looking around. The cloud was slowly passing through a vast canyon with mountain peaks on either side of him. He looked around, seeing trees peek out of and then disappear back into the clouds. A big brown eagle flew from one tree to another, giving a majestic screech that echoed off the sides of the mountain. A shaggy-haired ram with yellow horns curling up off the sides of his head stood on a rock, watching them as they drifted by. He bleated loudly, as if to say hello.

"Amazing," Matthew whispered to himself. Then, an idea struck him. "We're back on the ground!" he said louder, excited. "We're back on Earth! Maybe we can find somebody, we can—"

"Liam no! Stop it!"

"Let me go!"

Matthew turned around. Pete was grabbing his twin brother's arm, as he clung to the branch of a tree. Liam had been oddly silent during the discussion of missing their old lives on Earth. Now, Matthew was about to gain a clue as to why.

"We have to go home, Pete!" Liam yelled to his brother. "We have to see Mum and Dad! We can't let them keep thinking we did what we did!"

"Don't be a fool, Liam!" shouted back Pete angrily. "There's no going back! We've all promised each other never to make contact, even if we could. Isn't that right, Cal?" He looked to the Nubivagants' unofficial leader, who nodded solemnly. "Besides," Pete said, turning back to his brother. "We can't."

"We have to try!" Liam clung to the tree as the others slowly glided away on the cloud.

Pete let go of his brother's arm, upset. "Fine, try!" he shouted. "See how far you get! Say hello for me, will you?"

The others watched sadly as Liam began frantically climbing down the tree, disappearing under the surface of the cloud. "Shouldn't we do something?" Matthew gasped, concerned. "We're going to lose him!"

"No," Pete said quietly. "We're not."

Indeed, it wasn't but a minute later they saw Liam pop back up into the Sky. He dropped to his knees and buried his head in his hands, sobbing. Pete shook his head and walked over to him, embracing his brother. "I couldn't do it," Liam wept guiltily, as the mountain range faded into the distance, the Sky's brief interaction with the Earth now over. "I couldn't get anywhere."

"I know," Pete said, holding his twin tightly, tears coming to his own eyes. "I know, mate. It's okay."

"See?" Pam said sadly to Matthew. "There's no going back."

***

That night, Matthew had trouble falling asleep. The sight of Liam desperately trying to get back on the ground, back to his family, had rattled him. It was the first time things in the Sky seemed anything less than perfect. The thought of his parents down there on the ground, forced to live the rest of their lives without their beloved son, began to eat away at Matthew's happiness. He tossed and turned, restless and uneasy, until finally, he managed to fall into a deep, dreamless slumber.

15

From that day forward, Matthew found his thoughts returning to his parents more and more often. It was impossible to be as carefree as he once was, imagining them down there without him – especially considering the last encounter he'd had with them: that tense breakfast following the nasty exchange in which he had screamed and told them he hated them. Reflecting back on that memory now caused him an intense amount of guilt. It gave him a sharp little pain in his chest every time it crossed his mind. He wished so badly to somehow tell them he was okay, and that he was sorry for the hurt he caused them.

Then one day, in the midst of his mid-morning reveries, a remarkable occurrence happened to Matthew. It was an event that brought him right smack face to face with the life he had left behind so long ago.

The sun was almost completely overhead, after he had awoken and chatted with the others for awhile over a fresh helping of breakfast clouds. Having excused himself to take a stroll, Matthew now perched on the edge of the cloud, looking down at the Earth through Pam's telescope.

For many days now, the Sky had been floating along over the Pacific Ocean. Matthew didn't mind the times they were over this enormous body of water; he enjoyed the peacefulness of the silent waves beneath him. Once in awhile, he was lucky enough to catch sight of a school of dolphins jumping out of the sea – and he took special pleasure in knowing he was the only human being alive to witness that particular sight at that very second. But inevitably, after a few days, he would grow a bit bored of seeing only ocean, and begin to yearn to drift over land again. He preferred land, with all its mountains and buildings and people, scurrying around like multi-colored ants below.

So he was glad when he saw the edge of North America slowly creep into view from under the cloud he sat on. But he became really excited when he realized precisely where he was...floating directly over the San Francisco Bay Area!

In all the time he had been in the Sky, Matthew had never been fortunate enough to look down upon his hometown. The world was just so big, so enormously massive, the odds of his little patch of Sky passing over Tiburon were pretty small.

But now it was happening! Matthew looked down eagerly over the beautiful city of San Francisco. It was a clear day on the West Coast (his cloud being a harmless exception), there were dozens of sailboats in the bay, and countless people out in Golden Gate Park enjoying the sunshine. For once, Matthew was jealous of the folks down there. He wished he could jump down for an hour or two and share this gorgeous day with them.

Then he slowly drifted across the bay, and watched as the bright red Golden Gate Bridge passed underneath him. And lo and behold, a few minutes later, he was floating right over Tiburon. Looking down through the telescope, taking in all the sights of his youth he hadn't seen in so long, he held his breath, woozy with nostalgia.

There was his school, which he last saw when he was running away from Chad! How quickly he forgot that day since his adventures in the Sky. He trained the telescope on the students milling about outside. There were his classmates! He found it difficult to remember people's names, since he hadn't thought about them in ages, and hadn't been friends with a single one of them, of course. And yet the faces looked familiar – and older! It was such a strange feeling, as if he had taken a journey in a time machine. It boggled his mind, the concept that the world below had moved on without him, just as he had without it.

Then he saw the park his parents used to take him to play in when he was young, then the grocery store that was the scene of his last moments on Earth. And then, before he could even anticipate it, he was passing over his childhood house.

Matthew couldn't believe it. For the first time since the morning he'd left, he was looking at his very own home, the only one he ever knew before the Sky. A wave of warm tingles spread throughout his body. He didn't know quite what he was feeling...it was as if an incredible amount of joy and an incredible amount of sadness both came over him at the same time, fighting for space in his heart. It left him with a confusing feeling he would never be able to describe, had he been asked. He wondered if Pam ever felt the same floating over New York City.

Then, he noticed something else. In the backyard of his house, a man and a woman were standing on the grass, side by side, holding each other in an embrace. Their heads were bowed, so he couldn't see their faces, but it hit Matthew instantly, like a kick from a horse to his stomach, that he was looking down at his parents. At first they were unrecognizable. His mother, a little weary and weathered, was tightly clutching onto his father, as if she needed help to stand upright.

And then, a moment later, the cloud passed a bit further by, allowing him to see what his mom and dad were standing over. It was a gray slab, sticking straight up out of the backyard grass. It took Matthew a couple seconds to comprehend what he was looking at, but when he did, it suddenly left him gasping for air.

He was looking at his own grave.

16

Stunned, Matthew stared through the telescope at this surreal scene as long as he could, the cloud he sat upon drifting away, until a couple moments later, his house was completely out of sight. Then he dropped to his knees, clutching Pam's telescope to his chest, and began to cry.

Actually, that's not exactly accurate. Matthew wasn't crying – not like you or I have dozens of times, when our feelings are hurt, or when we stub our toe. This went beyond crying, or sobbing even. There were tears, yes, but Matthew was so upset, he literally lost control of his body. He lay on the cloud, unable to move, see, or even breathe. His body was attempting to take in air, but it was either taking in too much or not enough, it was difficult to tell. Either way, he was completely lost, both in mind and body, unable to process what he had just seen. That's when he felt something shaking him, and heard a distant voice fade up in his ear.

"Matthew! Matthew what's the matter? What's happened to you?"

Matthew opened his eyes, but it was still impossible to see anything. The Sky was swimming underneath the watery film of tears in his eyes. He tried to speak, but nothing came out besides a few upset grunts and gurgles.

"It's okay, mate. It's okay, just calm down. Just breathe a bit."

Matthew realized from the word "mate" and the kindness in his voice that it was Liam talking to him. This small discovery brought him back to the here and now, allowing him to calm down, if just a little bit. He managed to restore a somewhat regular breathing pattern.

"Good. Here, sit up. That's it." Liam gently guided Matthew up into a sitting position, at the same time carefully taking the telescope from him. "Now, tell me what's happened. Why you so upset?"

Matthew swallowed hard. "I saw them," he whispered hoarsely.

"Saw who?" Liam asked. Matthew turned his head slowly, looking him right in the eye.

"My parents," he replied. "My mom and dad."

"What d'you mean?" Liam asked, confused. "Like, in a dream? Were you having a nap?"

Matthew shook his head. "No," he said. "With the telescope. We were just passing over my town, where I'm from. I saw my own house, and in the yard, I saw my parents."

"That's incredible," said Liam, highly impressed. "That's fascinating. In fact, it's downright nearly impossible!" He began to get excited. "I mean, do you know the statistical probability of passing over your house at the exact moment you were looking down through this telescope?" he asked, holding Pam's prized possession up in the air. "And while your parents – two of about seven billion people on Earth – just happened to be standing outside? Why, it's got to be about one in a million! One in a billion! Actually, one in three-point-five billion!!! Matthew, this is a miracle! You should be overjoyed you got to see them, not upset!"

"You don't understand," Matthew said. "They were standing over a grave in the garden." He took a deep breath. "It was my grave. They think I'm dead."

Liam leaned back on his hands, exhaling a big sigh. "Oh, man," he said sympathetically. "I'm so sorry mate. That must be tough. That's awful."

"What am I going to do?" Tears began running down Matthew's cheeks all over again.

"There's nothing you can do, Matthew," said Liam softly. "You just have to try and forget about it."

"How can I forget about it? They're my parents. I can't bear the thought of them thinking I'm dead."

"Well..." Liam tried to be delicate with his words. "I mean...what did you think they thought?"

"Huh?" Matthew asked, looking at him.

"It's just...this whole time you've been up here, what did you think they thought had happened to you?"

"I don't know," Matthew admitted. "I guess maybe they just thought I...left, somehow, or...I don't know, I just...I didn't..."

"You're dead," said Liam matter-of-factly. "I mean, obviously you're not, but to them, to everyone down there..." Matthew just stared at him. "I know you don't want to think about this Matthew, but what you saw doesn't change anything. Your parents knew you floated away. It's the only thing that makes sense. In fact, there's no reason for them to think you *aren't* dead. I'm sure they've thought you dead for some time now."

Matthew looked at Liam, becoming upset with him. "You don't know that," he said. "You don't know when they decided to think that."

"Oh, come on!" shouted Liam, now even more upset than Matthew was. He started again, more aggressively. "At least you know *they're* okay! Do you know what I would give to be able to see my parents? To know they were alive and well down there without me and Pete? I mean, you don't know how unbelievably lucky you are!"

Matthew was shocked at how angry Liam had gotten so quickly. Liam was usually very mild-mannered and upbeat. Except, of course, for that one time he had tried to hold onto that tree...

"What happened to you and Pete?" he asked.

"What d'you mean?" replied Liam, wiping away some tears of his own.

"You never told me your story. How you guys got up here. Why don't either of you talk about it? Why does Pete hate the ground so much, and doesn't want us to have any contact with anybody down there? Why were you so desperate to go back that time we passed through the mountains?"

Liam looked down at the world passing silently below. Matthew waited expectantly. Then Liam took a slow deep breath, and began speaking softly.

"Pete and I were like you," he began. "We both floated from day one.

It's all we ever knew. But we didn't have anything like the gravity boots you had. We never got to walk, like normal people. Instead, our mum and dad got us wheelchairs."

"Oh," Matthew said, frowning. "That sounds..."

"Terrible," Liam finished Matthew's sentence for him. "It was like we were crippled. Not that there's anything wrong with that. I mean, if you are handicapped, if your legs don't work, then I suppose a wheelchair is a wonderful invention. It lets you get around when you otherwise wouldn't be able to. But our legs did work. And our parents were like yours; they made us promise to keep our floating a secret. So everyone thought there was something wrong with us – the weird cripple twins – and so that's how they treated us."

"They made fun of you," said Matthew, understanding.

"No, worse," said Liam. "They pitied us. We could see it in their faces, that they felt sorry for us. And every time someone looked at us that way, we just wanted to scream out, 'There's *nothing* wrong with us, you wanker! We're perfectly healthy, in fact, we're extraordinary! We're not bound by the law of gravity, like everyone else is! We're different, we're special, we're amazing!'" Liam closed his eyes, then said quietly, "But we couldn't."

Matthew didn't know what to say. His whole life, growing up, he didn't think any kid could have it worse than he did. But now he knew that wasn't true. At least his parents tried to find opportunities for him to live as "normal" a life as they could provide.

"Pete decided he couldn't take it anymore," Liam continued. "He told me he was going to leave, and he was going to do it with or without me." Now Liam began to cry as well. "I tried to talk him out of it for days, but his mind was made up. And in the end, I decided I couldn't let him do it alone. So on our twelfth birthday, we wrote a nice letter to our mum and dad, telling them we loved them. We got up early, before they did, got in our chairs, and snuck outside. And then, at the same time, we undid our seatbelts, and just..." He looked at Matthew and smiled sadly. "That was it."

Matthew was stunned with sadness for his friend. "My goodness, Liam," he said. "I had no idea. I'm so sorry."

"It's okay," Liam said. "I mean, obviously everything worked out great, as opposed to what we thought was going to happen. As opposed to what you thought was going to happen when those bullies took your boots. But...when I think of my parents, finding our empty chairs out there on the walk...yeah, mate. Let's just say I know how you feel."

Matthew nodded, thinking for a moment. "Do you ever regret it?" he asked. "Coming here, I mean. Even with everything we have, how wonderful it is...do you regret your decision?"

"Only when I think about my folks," Liam replied. "Only every day of my life."

17

A chill had crept over Matthew as he had listened to Liam's heartbreaking story. Now, he realized he actually felt quite cold, as the weather was starting to turn nasty. He noticed the cloud beneath his feet getting squishy with rain.

"I have to get to them somehow," he said to Liam, earnestly.

"Get to who?" Liam asked, confused.

"My parents!" Matthew exclaimed. "I have to let them know I'm all right somehow, that I'm not dead. I can't live with myself knowing that's what they think."

"Well if you couldn't live with yourself, then you really would be dead," Liam reminded him. "In which case, they'd be right."

"Liam," Matthew huffed, exasperated. "Knock it off, I'm serious!"

"I'm sorry, mate. But do you know what you are saying? There's no way to get to them. You know that. Stop torturing yourself."

Matthew racked his brain for ideas. "The airplanes," he suggested. "What if next time there's an airplane, we try and flag it down somehow?"

"Maybe," said Liam, reluctantly. "Seems awfully tricky though. A lot would have to happen for them to send someone up to find us, and that's even if they believed their own eyes. And besides..." Liam trailed off, looking over his shoulder to see if anyone else was nearby.

"Besides what?" Matthew prodded him. The wind was picking up. Matthew could feel the cloud oozing beneath him, as it began to rain on the world below.

"Well...you know the rules. We've all promised not to make contact under any circumstances. You made that promise too."

"I know, Liam, and I don't like to break promises, but come on!

Whose rule is it, anyway? Why does Pete get to call the shots around here?"

"Calvin too," Liam replied.

"Pete's filled Calvin's head with all sorts of ideas. He's scared him into believing that if we're found out, then bad things will happen. But that's not necessarily true. You know what I think?" Matthew stepped closer to Liam, lowering his voice. "I think Pete feels guilty. For what he made you do. For what he *did* do to your mom and dad. And I don't think he ever wants to face that."

Liam stared down at the clouds around them, which were getting grayer by the second. "You're right," said Liam. "He never talks about it. He's never mentioned it to me, not once since we arrived." He put his head down, now his turn to cry.

Matthew grabbed Liam in an embrace, giving him a much-needed hug. "There's got to be a way," he said, letting Liam go and looking him in the eyes. "There's got to be a way I can make things right with my parents...and you can make things right with yours."

Liam was still looking down at the clouds, sad, when he noticed something. "Gonna be a lightning storm," he said.

Matthew looked down, also seeing the early formations of the blue swirls starting to light up around them. He shrugged, unimpressed. "I'm too upset to enjoy it right now," he said.

But Liam kept staring at the swirls. He furrowed his brow, his mind working something out. "Lightning," he repeated. Then a second later, he looked up at Matthew, a spark in his eye. "Lighting! That's it!"

"What's it?" asked Matthew, getting excited too, but without knowing exactly why.

"Remember when the lightning sucked your robe right off your body?" Liam asked, smiling.

"Uh, yeah," said Matthew. "Unfortunately, I do."

"When the lightning strikes, it creates a vacuum," Liam explained. "It's so powerful, it takes all the air surrounding it down with it to the ground. So in order to fill that vacuum, everything anywhere near the lightning bolt —"

"Gets sucked down with it," Matthew finished Liam's sentence. Now he really was excited. "Liam, that's genius! I can literally ride the lightning down to Earth!"

"Well, in theory, yes," said Liam, suddenly nervous that Matthew had so quickly embraced his idea. "But it could be dangerous."

"Why? Would I get electrocuted?"

"No. I mean I don't think so. You have to be grounded to a surface for electricity to electrocute you. And even then, you wouldn't be actually touching the lightning anyway, technically. You'd just be following close behind it. Like hitching a ride on the back of it."

"Fantastic!" Matthew said. More lightning swirls were appearing now, as the storm was getting stronger. "What's the problem, then?"

"Well…" stammered Liam hesitantly. "I don't know. You'd be going very fast, and you could hit the ground at a very high speed. And if the lightning happened to strike something and cause a fire, well – you'd be in the middle of an explosion!"

"I have to take that chance," Matthew decided, already pacing around, looking for the next swirl forming. "Come on, help me find a good one."

"But you have no idea where you'll end up!" protested Liam, chasing after him.

"I don't care," Matthew said. "As long as I'm down there, I can get to them somehow. Aha!" He spotted a large blue swirl whirlpooling around about ten feet away, and ran over to it.

"But…but…the others!" Liam cried over the howl of the wind. He turned around, and saw Calvin, Pete, Pam and Antonella jogging towards them, waving, excited to watch the brewing lightning storm. He turned back to Matthew, who was now standing firmly atop the lightning swirl. "What

will I tell the others?"

Matthew looked up, his face bathed in the neon blue light of the massive lightning bolt crackling beneath him, just seconds away from exploding down across the sky.

"Tell them I had to do it," he said. "And that I love them."

Then, with Liam watching, with the other Nubivagants running over, their smiles turned to horror as they realized what they were witnessing. The cloud opened up beneath Matthew. A giant, magnificent lightning bolt streaked away, over the rain-soaked land thousands of feet below.

In an instant, Matthew was sucked straight down out of the Sky, screaming at the top of his lungs, riding the lightning back to the world he had left behind.

PART III: THE RETURN

1

Matthew would probably not be able to describe to you the experience of coming down out of the Sky. One moment he was up in the clouds, and the next he was underwater, consumed by a freezing coldness that shocked his system and sent his nerves and brain into a frenzy. What happened in between was, in the most literal sense, a blur.

If Matthew had not traveled quite at the speed of light, then he had not been too far off. It was too short a time to even think about what was happening, much less react. The lightning bolt zigged and zagged its way downward, finally finishing its journey about a hundred feet above the dark, churning waters of the San Francisco Bay, before vanishing into the air. Matthew followed right behind in its path, without actually touching it. When the lightning disappeared, and with it the vacuum-like force pulling him through the air, his momentum carried him even further. And so down he went, plunging deep into the icy bay.

Now he was underwater, too dazed to process what had just happened. But when he finally came to a stop, Matthew realized he could not breathe, and began to panic. It was extremely dark; in fact, he couldn't see anything, and found it difficult to even know which way was up. Luckily, his floating kicked in – more so than that of a regular person, of course – and he quickly began rising towards the surface. To speed up the process, Matthew began kicking, forcing himself upwards as rapidly as he could.

Seconds later he broke the surface of the water, taking in great big gulps of air. He breathed heavily for a few minutes, gasping, as heavy rain pelted down upon his head and the surrounding water. It took him a minute to determine that he was not injured.

Then, it struck him that he was not floating away, back up into the air!

He thought back to when he was much younger, and his mom used to give him baths in the tub. *Incredible*, Matthew thought to himself, bobbing along the water's surface. *The water keeps me from floating away, the same way the clouds do in the Sky.*

Suddenly, Matthew realized he was freezing cold, and a moment later, he became terribly frightened. It had been a jarring couple of minutes. When he had left the Sky, he had no idea where he would end up. But floating in the middle of a vast, dark, icy body of water was about as scary a place as he could have predicted. He looked around, frantically searching for something, anything, to give him a clue as to where he was.

And then he saw one: off in the distance were the bright, shining, unmistakable lights of the San Francisco skyline. In fact, the words "Port of San Francisco" lit up the famous Ferry Building in big red neon, probably only a couple miles away.

"I'm home!" Matthew shouted to himself, in the middle of the downpour. "I did it! I'm home!" But then, he realized he was in fact a couple miles away...an impossible distance for most people to swim in the choppy waters of the San Francisco Bay, but especially a young boy.

The adrenaline of the ride down was quickly wearing off. The frigid cold of the water was rapidly seeping through his skin and into his bones. Matthew could feel his arms and legs going numb, and realized within seconds he probably wouldn't even be able to use them to swim.

As if right on cue, he heard the sudden whir of a machine coming up behind him. He whirled his head around. Coming straight at him out of the darkness was a boat. Matthew stared up at it in awe, growing excited over the prospect of being rescued. Then he realized whoever was manning this boat must not have seen him in the water below, because the boat was showing no signs of slowing down as it plowed towards Matthew, full speed ahead.

2

Just as it looked as if the boat might run right over him, unceremoniously doing him in just minutes after his glorious return to planet Earth, Matthew screamed and ducked down under the water, narrowly avoiding what would have been a gruesome fate.

However, thanks to his floating, he wasn't able to stay underwater more than a couple seconds, and he bobbed back up to the surface, his head bumping against the underside of the boat. "Urg," Matthew groaned to himself, releasing precious air into the water. Frightened, he put his hands up, and could feel the boat bottom cruising past him. Instinctively, he closed his fingers, trying to grab hold of something, anything – and unlike when he was floating away from the supermarket and up into the sky, this time he got lucky.

He caught hold of a metal bar on the back of the boat, and managed to hang on as he floated up behind it. He sucked in oxygen as the boat pulled him along the bay. Then, he turned himself over onto his belly, grabbed onto the bar with his other hand, and began pulling himself up.

It wasn't easy, but using all his strength, Matthew was able to get his feet up on the bar. From there, he could extend upwards, and got an arm up and over the back railing of the boat. It was a rather small vessel, so there wasn't much distance between the boat's deck and the water. Once he had a secure grip, Matthew grunted and pulled and managed to heave himself up and over the railing, landing on the slick wet deck with a thud.

Once out of the water, he immediately felt his body floating up into the air again. He held tightly to the railing, taking a minute to carefully get his footing as the boat bobbed and jumped over the choppy water. When he was fairly confident he wasn't going to float away, Matthew took stock of his circumstances.

The most immediate problem he discovered was that he was naked. Somewhere along the journey down out of the Sky, he had lost his cloud-clothes – which really should come as no surprise, because surely anything made of cloud would be expected to dissolve in water. Nevertheless, Matthew felt he should solve this problem before moving on.

Luckily, he saw a coat rack just across the deck, attached to the outer wall of the boat's main cabin, just a few feet from where he was holding himself down with the railing. And on the coat rack was exactly what he needed: raincoats.

Matthew attempted to reach the coats while still holding onto the railing, but he was about six inches short. Perhaps in a couple years, when he was a little bit taller, and his arms a little bit longer, he would've been able to reach the raincoats without breaking contact from the railing. But at this particular moment in time, no matter how far he tried to extend his fingers, he just wasn't going to be able to get one of those coats. Not without breaking away from the railing.

It was a risk he was going to have to take, if he wanted to cover up – a necessity, he felt, for when he inevitably came across another person. It was such a short distance, the space between his fingertips and the raincoats. And yet, if anything went wrong...if the boat jostled him at just the wrong moment, and he happened to miss, for whatever reason...well, it was enough to give him pause, making sure he was absolutely ready.

So he took a deep breath, steeling himself. "You got this," he said to himself out loud. Then he gave himself a countdown. "One...two...three!" Matthew pushed off the deck railing, jettisoning himself towards the raincoats. He slammed into the cabin wall, grabbing a raincoat in the process, but then felt himself begin to move upwards. "Ah!" he shouted, managing to grab onto one of the metal hooks of the coat rack. Planting his feet on the wall, he steadied himself, and was able to use his free hand to shimmy one raincoat sleeve over his arm. He swung the coat over his back, then switched hands, grabbing the hook with one, and sliding the other down the second sleeve.

"Yes!" Matthew congratulated himself, now protected from the elements with a dark green rain slicker, whose only negative was that it was grownup size, and thus much too large for him. But other than that: mission accomplished.

"Hey!" a gruff voice shouted at Matthew through the rain, interrupting his private celebration. Still clinging to the coat rack, his feet up against the wall like a rock climber, Matthew turned and saw a large, burly man standing on the deck just a few feet away, wearing a similar raincoat, his face looking surprised and angry. "What are you doing on my boat?"

Petrified, Matthew opened his mouth to answer, but could only squeak out a measly "Hi."

The man walked slowly over to Matthew, eyes glaring at him, water dripping menacingly from his bushy black beard. "A stowaway, huh?" He looked Matthew up and down, taking in the oversized raincoat. "A stowaway thief!"

"No," Matthew began to protest. "No, you don't understand—"

The scary man suddenly gripped Matthew's arm, hard, and shouted in his face "Don't lie to me, boy!" His heavy breath felt hot against Matthew's chilly face, as he growled, "Get inside."

3

A moment later, the bearded, burly man held Matthew firmly by the backs of both arms, marching him down the deck to the door of the cabin. In one fell swoop, he opened the door and shoved Matthew inside.

Matthew skidded across the floor of the small room. He could feel his feet begin to rise up into the air. He desperately did not want to give himself away so soon, especially since he had already gotten on this guy's bad side. Thinking fast, he pitched himself forward towards a little passenger bench, grabbed hold of a pair of seat belt straps, pulled himself down onto the bench, and secured the seatbelt across his lap. He pulled the end as tight as it would go, locking his bottom down to the bench, then planted his feet on the floor and looked up at the lumbering, angry grownup scowling down at him.

"What are you doing on my boat?" the man roared. "Can't a fisherman make an honest living without worrying about little riff-raffians stowing away and stealing his ten dollar raincoats?!"

"I'm sorry, sir!" Matthew said pleadingly. "I'm not a stowaway! I was in the water, and your boat almost ran me over! I grabbed the back and climbed on, just now. I'm sorry about the raincoat, I...I lost my clothes." Matthew looked down sheepishly at his feet.

"You little liar," the fisherman growled. "You expect me to believe you were just floating around San Francisco Bay in the middle of a thunderstorm, and my little boat just happened to pass by you, at which point you just grabbed hold and climbed aboard?"

"Y-yeah," Matthew said, trembling with fear. "That's what happened, sir."

"I see," said the fisherman, stroking his beard. "And just what, may I ask, were you doing out here?"

"Well...uh..." Matthew stalled, trying to come up with a believable reason for his predicament. "Uh...well...I could ask you the same question! What are *you* doing out here in the middle of a storm?"

"I'm a fisherman!" cried the fisherman. "These are the best conditions to catch fish! Besides, I have a boat!" He folded his arms, looking down at him. "Fess up, kid. Or else I'm gonna put you right back in the water...and I'm keeping my raincoat!"

Matthew sighed. "Please, sir. I...I need to get home to my parents. They live in Tiburon. I've been away a long time, and they're probably very worried about me. Do you mind just giving them a call? They can pick me up at the dock, and then I'll be out of your hair. I'm very sorry for any trouble I've caused you." He looked up at the fisherman, and tried his best attempt at an innocent expression. "Please?"

The fisherman's face softened a bit. "What did you do, run away from home?" he asked.

"Something like that," said Matthew.

The fisherman studied Matthew's face for a minute. He couldn't quite put his finger on it...but something about it looked a little familiar. His gaze then traveled down the rest of Matthew's body, resting on his feet, which were dangling in the air. Wait – were they dangling? Or did it look more like they were…?

Matthew also looked down at his own feet, which he had forgotten to keep pressed against the floor, and were now aimlessly drifting up into the air. He quickly realized his mistake, and slammed them down onto the floor strangely, looking back up at the fisherman with a nervous laugh.

"I see," said the fisherman, eyeing the boy suspiciously. Then he walked over to his captain's chair, in front of the steering wheel and a bank of buttons and controls. "Well, I don't have a phone on the boat. But I'll radio the dock and tell them to have a taxi waiting. That way you'll be able to get wherever you want to go. That good enough for you?"

Matthew smiled, relieved. "Oh thank you sir!" he gushed. He couldn't believe he'd convinced the fisherman to help him. "My name's Matthew, by the way."

"Charlie Callahan," said the fisherman, picking up the microphone of his CB radio. "Pleased to meet you." Then he pushed the talk button and spoke into it. "This is Charlie Callahan to Tiburon Station, do you read me? Over." There was a pause, during which Matthew heard a loud crackle of static, before another man's voice came over the radio.

"Tiburon Station, we read you Mr. Callahan. Over."

"Yeah, I've got a Code 45 out here. Requesting assistance when I dock in about, oh..." He checked his wristwatch. "Twenty minutes."

There was another pause. "Did you say Code 45?" asked the voice, sounding somewhat surprised.

"Yes sir," replied Charlie Callahan casually. "Can you provide assistance?"

"Uh, yes, of course Mr. Callahan," answered the voice. "We'll be ready for you."

"Great," said Charlie. "See you soon. Over and out." He turned back to Matthew and smiled. "All good," he said.

"Wonderful, thank you so much!" said Matthew, being careful to keep his feet firmly on the floor. "What's a Code 45? Is that what you say when you need a taxi?"

The fisherman flashed another smile at Matthew, this one making him more than a bit uneasy, and said, "Something like that."

4

For the next twenty minutes or so, Matthew sat on the bench in the fishing boat's small cabin, which contained very little other than fishing equipment, a miniature refrigerator, and some old fishing magazines. He was very excited, as well as very nervous. Something about the exchange between Charlie Callahan and the man on the radio had unsettled him. And now, the fisherman wasn't saying anything; he just manned the steering wheel, piloting the boat over the bumpy waves of the water. Not that Matthew particularly wanted to make small talk; it was just that the silence made him even more nervous than he already was.

Eventually, Matthew looked out the windshield and could see the lights of the shore approaching. The boat slowed down and began bobbing up and down slowly, as the fisherman steadily aimed the nose of the boat towards the dock.

"Here we are," the man said, glancing at Matthew before returning to the business of bringing the boat in.

"We're here," Matthew said to himself. Then, louder: "We're here! I'm going home! I'm going..." His voice trailed off as the lights from the dock became more visible. They were red and blue, swirling around and around. Beneath them, Matthew could make out the silhouette of a police car.

"That's not a taxi," Matthew said softly.

"Sorry kid," shot back Charlie, even though his voice didn't sound like he was sorry at all. "Your story just seemed a little too suspicious to let you run off into the night by yourself."

"No," Matthew protested, becoming very anxious. "Please, you can't let them take me! Just let me call my parents, please!"

"It's too late, kid." The boat pulled up alongside a wooden dock.

Within seconds, there was a loud knocking on the cabin door. Before Charlie could open it, two policemen burst in. "Hey, take it easy!" Charlie complained. "Those hinges ain't as strong as they used to be."

The cops ignored the fisherman, their eyes falling immediately upon Matthew. "Holy cow," the taller one said, his eyes going wide. "Is that the kid?"

"I don't believe it," said the other one, who was shorter and fatter. "You're the Mitchell kid, aren't you? The one who's been missing over a year now?"

Matthew nodded. "I need to go home," he said, tears welling in his eyes.

The cops looked at each other, then started unbuckling Matthew's seatbelt. Afraid of what might happen if they discovered he could float, he quickly threw his arms around the fatter cop, and did his best to sound frightened. "Please, don't let me go! Take me home, please!"

The fat cop was taken aback a bit. He looked at his partner, who just shrugged. "All right, kid. Take it easy. We'll get you home," he said, patting Matthew's back. They started walking off the boat onto the dock.

"Hey!" Charlie Callahan called after them. "How about a little appreciation? No thank you?"

"Thank you very much, sir," replied the taller policeman over his shoulder as he walked down the dock. "We appreciate your assistance."

"What about my raincoat?!" the fisherman cried. But by that time, Matthew had no chance to respond. Because just as the cops got to their car, a big white van with an oversized logo on the door and a satellite on its roof came screeching up to the dock.

Out hopped a guy holding a big camera on his shoulder, and a woman with her hair and makeup done up like she was about to be on TV – which, of course, she was.

"Go, go, go! Roll it!" the woman shouted at the cameraman. He flipped a switch, and a bright spotlight lit up atop the camera.

"We're rolling!" the cameraman shouted back.

The newswoman held a microphone to her mouth and spoke into the camera. "I'm Tracey Tish, live at the Tiburon dock, where we've just gotten word that missing boy Matthew Mitchell has miraculously surfaced in – of all places – the San Francisco Bay, after being missing for well over a year!" She turned to the policemen, who seemed caught off guard, and Matthew, who seemed terrified. "Young man, are you in fact Matthew Mitchell? Where have you been this whole time? Are you all right?"

Matthew stared into the camera, mouth hanging open, squinting because of the bright light in his eyes. Before he had a chance to say anything, the taller cop said sternly to the reporter, "No questions right now." He quickly opened the back door of the police car, and the policeman holding Matthew hurriedly placed him in the back seat and slammed the door shut.

Matthew quickly buckled himself in as the cops got in the front seats and started the engine. He peered out the window at the reporter, who was still shouting questions at him through the glass, the camera still aimed at his face. He stared at her, speechless, mouth agape, as the police siren blared loudly and the car sped away, red and blue light bathing the darkness outside.

5

While Matthew had been riding a lightning bolt down to Earth, climbing aboard a fishing vessel, and being turned over to the Tiburon police department, his parents had been getting ready to go to bed, less than a mile away.

Daniel and Allison Mitchell did not have very much variety in their lives these days. Having never really moved on from Matthew's disappearance – death, in their minds – their personalities had undergone a change. They had grown sad, and old – not in years, necessarily, but in spirit. It was unfortunate, really, but who could blame them? There aren't many fates in life worse than losing a child.

So as an older, somewhat boring couple, they spent the vast majority of their evenings the exact same way: they ate dinner in hushed conversations, changed into their pajamas, got into bed and fell asleep while watching television.

They usually liked to watch the local news, followed by a late night talk show. And this night was no different. So after brushing their teeth and washing their faces, they tucked themselves in and flipped on the TV. But what came on their screen this particular night was definitely out of the ordinary.

It was a "Special Live Report," accompanied by exciting music and flashy, colorful graphics. The news anchor, a handsome man with an impressive head of silver hair, told the viewers they were about to see exclusive Channel 8 footage of breaking news – a child had turned up in the middle of the bay, and there was reason to believe it was local boy Matthew Mitchell, who had gone missing some time ago.

At the mention of his name, the flesh on Daniel and Allison's arms, necks and backs almost completely transformed from smooth human skin into rigid, goose-pimpled hides. Chills shot both up *and* down their spines, and they instinctively sat up and leaned closer to their television set.

What followed was Tracey Tish's brief but hair-raising report. When she directed the camera towards the policeman holding Matthew, and Matthew turned his head and looked into the camera, Allison and Daniel simultaneously became breathless. Allison screamed out a brief, shrill noise, and gripped Daniel's arm so hard, it would leave a bruise that lasted about two weeks. But Daniel did not even feel it as he stared at the TV, mouth wide open, tears instantly streaming down his face.

After they watched Matthew being put in the police car and driven away, and the footage cut back to the news anchor saying "We will bring you more developments as they unfold," Daniel and Allison looked at each other. Both of them were having some difficulty processing what they had just seen on their bedroom TV. It felt very much like a dream, a version of the same dream both of them had had a thousand times since they had last seen their son. They weren't quite sure if this was real, and were afraid to say anything that might cause it not to be.

But after only a few seconds, Allison took that risk. "He's alive," she whispered.

"He's alive," Daniel whispered back.

They both leapt out of bed.

6

The police car pulled into the police station parking lot. Now that Channel 8 had aired their breaking news story, the rest of the local stations had sent their news teams out to cover the story as well. The return of a missing local boy was big news, and no one wanted to miss out on the action. So when Matthew arrived at the station, there was a whole cluster of news vans, cameramen and reporters waiting for him.

Before the car even came to a stop, these reporters were peering into the window, shouting questions at him. The policemen quickly got out and yelled at them all to back off, to "Give the boy some space!" before they opened Matthew's door. "Come on out, son," said the tall cop. "It's all right, we got you."

Matthew just stared back at him, frightened. He was overwhelmed, of course, but he was also mindful that he could not just exit the car like a normal person. So instead, he tried to stall as best he could. "I can't," he said feebly.

"Why not?" asked the cop.

"Uh...my foot's asleep."

"Come on, kid, shake it off," said the pudgy cop nervously. "We don't want you out here in front of these cameras."

"It really hurts," Matthew said, reaching down and massaging his right foot. "Can I just wait in the car for a few minutes?"

The cops looked at each other, exasperated. "It's too late for this," said the fat one. "I gotta get home to Barb, or she's gonna blow her stack."

The taller one sighed, turning to Matthew. "Come on, buddy," he said, reaching in to unbuckle his seatbelt.

"No, wait!" Matthew protested. There was a click, and Matthew felt

himself rise up into the air a bit. He quickly grabbed hold of the policeman, wrapping his arms around his neck as the cop pulled him out of the car.

"Jeez, kid, come on!" he complained. "Here, I'm just gonna set you down right here, and we'll walk into the station together, okay?"

He leaned down, trying to place Matthew onto the ground. Matthew felt his feet touch the asphalt of the parking lot. The cop began removing Matthew's arms from around his neck. "Wait!" Matthew screamed, afraid that in another second, his entire, brief journey down to Earth would be over. "Don't let me go! If you do, I'll fl—"

Just then the screech of tires drowned out the rest of Matthew's statement. Everyone turned and looked as Daniel and Allison jumped out of their car and ran over to him, past the crush of reporters. "Matthew!" Allison cried. "Matthew, is that really you?"

"Mom! Dad!" Matthew yelled back. The fatter policeman momentarily tried to stop his parents from coming towards him, but then thought better of it. They were not to be stopped. When they were about three feet away, Matthew let go of the cop, pushing himself in his parents' direction. He flew through the air, right into their arms, the three of them squeezing each other tightly and bawling with happiness.

It was a sight captured by every news camera on the scene, and within minutes would be broadcast on practically every channel throughout the country. A long lost boy had been reunited with his parents. Matthew was home.

7

The sensations felt by Matthew's parents as they held their son again, having long ago given up hope he would ever return, were the most joyful known to mankind. Not only the sight of Matthew, but every sense they possessed was overwhelmed and overjoyed, all at the same time. The smell of his hair. The sound of his voice. And of course, the feel of his arms around them. In those first few moments of reuniting with their child, Daniel and Allison felt just about every emotion a person is capable of experiencing. They were the happiest people on Earth (or in the Sky, for that matter).

Matthew was just as overcome, seeing his beloved mom and dad again. But for him it was a slight bit different. He knew he had been alive this whole time; they did not. And he had been preparing for this moment mentally for over an hour now. They were taken completely by surprise. They could hardly wrap their minds around his being there, and kept giving him sideways glances in the fear he may disappear again.

"Where have you been?" Daniel asked, as he pulled away slightly to look into his son's face.

"We thought you were..." Allison began crying, unable to even say it. "We thought we'd lost you."

"Where did you go?" Daniel asked again.

"We need to get you inside," the taller policeman said, nervously eyeing the television cameras, which were capturing the entire reunion.

"I want to go home," said Matthew. "Can't we just go home?"

"Not quite yet," said the cop. "You're a missing boy, we can't just let you leave."

"Why not?" Allison demanded, growing irritated. "We're his parents.

Why can't we take him home?"

"Well," stammered the policeman, not 100% sure what the correct answer was. "We need to take a statement. There's paperwork to fill out. Right?" he turned to his pudgy partner, looking for backup.

"Oh. Yeah, right," the shorter cop confirmed. "There's a protocol for this sort of thing, I'm sure."

"All right, all right," Daniel said. "It's okay. You'll just answer some questions, and then we'll go home, okay?"

"Okay," said Matthew. Daniel and Allison began to lower him to the ground, but he gripped their arms, and whispered, "Wait!" into their ears. "You can't let me go!"

His parents looked at each other knowingly, somewhat dismayed this was still, after all this, something to worry about. "Wait here," Daniel said, passing his son over to the taller cop. "Hold onto him tight. I'll be right back." Then he ran back over to their car. He popped open the trunk, grabbed something, slammed down the trunk top, then jogged back over.

Daniel kneeled down in front of the policeman holding Matthew. In his hands he held a plastic grocery bag. And out of the bag, he pulled Matthew's old pair of gravity boots. "We kept these," he said, looking up at Matthew. "Just in case. Someone left them on our doorstep the day after you went missing."

Matthew looked at the gravity boots, feeling mixed emotions. On the one hand, they would allow him to safely walk on the ground again. On the other...the sight of them brought back some not-too-fond memories.

But Daniel was already placing Matthew's left foot, then his right, into the boots. He buckled them in, then turned them on. The familiar green light appeared on the heel, and Matthew felt them pull gently towards the ground. He looked at the cop who was holding him. "You can put me down now," he said.

Confused as to what exactly was happening, the cop gently lowered

Matthew to the ground. "Thanks," Matthew said. Then he looked up at his parents, taking them each by the hand. "Come on," he said. "Let's go inside."

8

Matthew and his parents were released from the police station fairly quickly. Once the police were able to confirm Daniel and Allison were in fact his parents, and that he was in good health, they had no real reason to keep him there. Ideally, they would have liked to interview him extensively to find out exactly what had happened to him, and where he had been this whole time. They would have needed to know if there were any kidnappers, any other people involved, but of course Matthew could not tell them the truth – not without getting into a whole mess of having to reveal his floating. So, with the help of his mom and dad, he insisted he was very tired, and just wanted to go home and be with his family for now. And in the end, the cops didn't have much choice but to let them go.

Once they were home, after Matthew had gotten over the extremely weird feeling of walking around his old house again, the three of them sat in the living room, and Matthew told his parents everything. For the next few hours, deep into the night, Daniel and Allison hung on Matthew's every word, scarcely able to believe their own ears.

He began with that day at school over a year ago, when he pushed Chad Gregory, who then chased him with his two goons. He described how they cornered him behind the supermarket, held him down and forcibly removed his gravity boots. He told them about floating away into the sky, and how he was certain those were the final moments of his life. He told them about how he got dizzy as he saw the world disappearing beneath him, and that everything finally went black. And he told them about waking up in what he assumed must have been heaven. "But it wasn't heaven," he explained. "It was the Sky."

Matthew's parents sat on the edge of their seats, listening with wonderment and disbelief as Matthew described this whole other world that existed up in the clouds, populated only by the Nubivagants – a group of kids who were just like him. He told them all about Calvin, the twins, Pam and Antonella. He told them about eating the clouds, and hiding from airplanes, and watching the world pass by below them.

Then Matthew came to the difficult part of his story, of having to describe what it was like to look down through Pam's telescope and see his parents standing above his grave in their backyard, just a few hours ago. He began to choke up, which in turn caused his mom and dad to start crying. "Matthew," Allison wept, "I'm so sorry...we thought...we were certain..."

"We had no idea about any of this," Daniel said, equally emotional. "I'm so sorry, Matthew, I'm so sorry."

"It's okay," Matthew said, wiping tears from his eyes. "How could you have known? I just felt so awful. Because even from miles above, I could see how sad you were. And I thought I would never be able to tell you I was okay."

"So then...how did you do it?" asked Allison. "How did you come back?"

Matthew's eyes lit up. "That's the coolest part," he grinned, and told them about riding the lightning down into the bay. His mom squeezed her husband's arm and put a hand over her heart, horrified.

"Matthew Mitchell!" she exclaimed. "That's the most dangerous thing I can ever imagine! Don't you ever ride a lightning bolt ever again!"

"Shhh, let him finish!" said Daniel, impressed with his son's courage and enraptured by his story. "Go on, son," he said, leaning forward.

Matthew continued on, describing the freezing waters, almost getting run over by the boat, climbing aboard, getting caught "borrowing" Charlie's raincoat, and the tense interrogation that followed. He finished up by telling of the ride into the Tiburon dock and being surprised by the police waiting for him, then riding back to the station and getting out of the car, which is where Daniel and Allison themselves entered the story. "That pretty much sums it up," Matthew said, his voice a bit tired after several hours of speaking. "The rest of it you were here for."

His parents were absolutely astounded. "Incredible," Daniel said. "Unbelievable," said Allison. There was a beat of silence, as nobody knew quite what to say next.

But then Matthew had a question. "That grave in the backyard," he said. "My grave. Did you guys go out there every single day?"

"No," his mother said quietly. "Just today."

"Why today?" asked Matthew.

"You don't know...?" Allison said, bewildered, her voice trailing off. "Of course you don't," she then said. "How could you, after all this time?"

"Know what?" asked Matthew.

"Matthew," his dad said, taking his hand. "Today is your thirteenth birthday." Matthew stared at them.

"It is?"

"Happy birthday, baby," his mother said, going over and hugging him. His father wrapped both of them in his arms.

"Happy birthday, Matthew." Matthew suddenly felt very strange. How odd it was to have to be told that it was his birthday! A birthday is something you look forward to for days, if not weeks, leading up to it! It's not a day that just sneaks up on you in this sort of manner.

"I'm thirteen," he said. "But...I didn't even get to be twelve."

"You left just before your last one," his mom explained.

"Huh," Matthew said, processing the bizarre sensation of having skipped over an entire age without realizing it. "So I'm a teenager now?"

"You're a teenager, buddy. Congratulations," his dad said, shaking his hand.

Then another, somewhat chilling thought crossed Matthew's mind. "So if I had looked down on any other day, you probably wouldn't have been out there," he said.

"No, most likely not," answered his mom.

"I wouldn't have seen you. So then I probably wouldn't have..." He swallowed, the hair on the back of his neck prickling up.

His mother saw what he was getting at, and she rubbed his shoulders soothingly. "Don't think that way, sweetie," she said. "Everything happens for a reason."

"It's so late," Daniel said, checking his watch. "We should probably get to bed. I imagine we're all exhausted. Especially you, birthday boy," he said, ruffling his son's hair.

A few minutes later, Matthew was back in his old bedroom, marveling at how everything looked the exact same as when he last saw it. It felt as if he had never left.

He sat on the bed and quickly noticed how loud and stiff it was compared to his more recent sleeping arrangements. He started to take off his gravity boots, but his parents immediately stopped him. "I don't think that's a good idea, Matthew," said his mom.

"I agree," said Daniel. "Why don't you just leave those on for now?"

"For good," insisted Allison, nervousness in her voice. "I don't want you ever taking those off, Matthew. Do you understand?"

Matthew stared up at his parents, suddenly very uneasy. "I don't need to wear them to bed," he protested. "There's no way for me to float away while I'm in my bedroom."

"Just wear them. For my sake," said his mother. "Tonight, at least. Just let me go to sleep knowing you're here, and you're one hundred percent safe. Please?"

Matthew nodded. "Okay, Mom," he said. "I'll wear them tonight."

"Thank you," she said. Then she and Daniel kissed and hugged him a few more times, before ultimately tearing themselves away and going down the hall to their bedroom, to sleep easily for the first time since before

Matthew had departed.

On the other hand, Matthew did not sleep all that well himself. He was incredibly happy to see his parents again, and so relieved they knew he was alive and well. The burden of their sorrow had been lifted from his shoulders, and for that he was extremely grateful.

And yet, as he lay in his old bed, weighed down by the stifling gravity boots on his feet, Matthew couldn't help but feel uncomfortable. As he eventually drifted off into a fitful sleep, he noticed some unpleasant memories of his childhood creeping back into his mind.

9

Over the next couple weeks, Matthew experienced the very unique and strange process of readjusting to a life he had spent considerable time away from. And, as many returning war heroes could probably tell you, it's not nearly as easy as you might think.

He was happy to be home, of course; he was overjoyed to be reunited with his family. That practically goes without saying. And his parents simply could not stop smiling, pretty much every second of every day – even when they were asleep! They truly felt as if their son had been reborn, like they had a second chance at being parents. You'll find, as you get older, that the best, happiest experiences are often not necessarily when something good happens to you, but the avoidance of something bad. So when Matthew returned to their lives, and they learned that their son was not dead but very much alive, well – that was without question the happiest moment in both of their lives, a high they were nowhere close to coming down from anytime soon.

Publicly, there was a frenzy of attention regarding Matthew's return. It was the beginning of summer; school had let out the following week. Nevertheless, everyone in town quickly became aware of the fact that the local boy, the one who had been missing for so long, the one whose poor parents had gone on TV and pleaded for anyone with knowledge of his whereabouts to please come forward, had suddenly returned, long after everyone had given up hope.

And what was even stranger was that he and his parents were being so mysteriously coy about where he had been the entire time. He wasn't hurt; he didn't appear to have been kidnapped, or abducted by aliens. Television shows, newspaper reporters, and even the police could not seem to get any shred of information out of the Mitchell family as to what happened to him. Daniel and Allison simply told them all that their son was back and in perfect health, and that was all that mattered. Beyond that, they smiled and simply asked that everyone please respect their privacy.

Of course, this was all part of a well-coordinated plan on behalf of the Mitchells. Daniel and Allison still were adamantly opposed to outsiders learning that Matthew did not obey they law of gravity – perhaps now more than ever. And for his part, Matthew did not want to tell anybody outside of his parents about the Sky, or the other Nubivagants. He remembered their concerns about being found out, and the oath they had made him take (which he had broken, of course, by returning to Earth), and he did not want to risk exposing them. No, he determined, the story of where he had been this whole time would simply have to remain a mystery to the outside world.

But then, after all the commotion had died down, Matthew found it kind of difficult to just go back to his old life. Putting on those boots every morning was something he found hard to get used to again. Every time he clicked that latch down over his feet, a pin-prickly sensation immediately materialized in the pit of his stomach and began spiderwebbing throughout the rest of his body, like a crack in a car windshield, eventually reaching the temples of his forehead and causing a dull pounding headache.

There was something else that began to bother Matthew more and more as well, and that was that even though his parents were so thrilled to have him back home, they had also made up their minds that they were going to take no chances when it came to the potential of losing him again. As such, they tried their darndest to be around him as often as they could. They never went out together without bringing him along, and they absolutely forbade him to leave the house by himself.

Now, these restrictions would be difficult for any teenage boy to tolerate. But Matthew found it especially claustrophobic considering he had just spent the last great big chunk of his life being as free as he could possibly imagine. He did not like being constantly watched, monitored, parented. And he especially did not like wearing those confining gravity boots, which disgusted him more and more with each passing day, their black heaviness weighing him down, both physically and mentally.

"Mom," he complained one day, a little over a month after he had returned. "I just want to go to the store to get a comic book," he sighed wearily.

"All right, so I'll take you," Allison said, getting up from the kitchen table, where she had been reading a book. "Just let me put on a sweater."

"I don't need you to take me," protested Matthew. "It's a half mile away!"

"We talked about this, Matthew. I'm not letting you out of my sight."

"What are you going to do?" Matthew said, his voice rising with irritation. "You can't follow me around for the rest of my life!"
Allison stopped and stared at him, raising one eyebrow.

"Don't take that attitude with me, young man," she said. "You just came back. So if you think your father and I are going to risk something like that happening again, you've got another thing coming."

A few minutes later, Matthew was riding in the car next to his mother, wondering if he was as happy to be back on Earth as he had initially thought he was.

10

Matthew walked into the supermarket, his mother holding his hand to be even more on the safe side, which just made him all the more frustrated (after all, what 13-year-old boy wants to hold hands with his mom, especially out in public?). But given that this supermarket happened to be the exact same spot from where Matthew had floated away, she simply wasn't going to take any chances. So Matthew had little choice other than to grumble and deal with it.

They went over to the magazine racks, where Matthew looked over the comic books. Having spent much of the last few weeks at home without a lot to do, he had recently grown quite fond of reading comic books. The flying superheroes reminded him of a certain freedom he found himself missing lately, so comics allowed him to experience a bit of that escape once again.

After picking out a couple cool looking ones, Allison again took his hand, leading him down the aisle. "I just want to stop by the meat department," she said. "I thought I might make chicken Parmesan tonight. How does that sound?"

But Matthew wasn't listening. In fact, he had stopped walking entirely, his face gone pale, his blood cold.

"Matthew, what is it?" Allison asked, looking down at him. But when he failed to answer, she looked ahead to what he was staring at: a stock boy, roughly Matthew's age, at the end of the aisle, stocking the store shelves with cans of soup.

The boy was Chad Gregory.

He was a bit older now, obviously. But that didn't prevent Matthew from recognizing him instantly. And being so unprepared for this run-in, he had absolutely no idea what to do with his mouth, his eyes, his hands, all of which seemed to have detached their lines of communication from his brain.

His mother, of course, did not understand what the problem was. "Matthew," she said again, louder this time. "What is wrong with you?"

Almost as if it was happening in slow motion, Chad began to turn and look in Matthew's direction. And from deep within his brain, Matthew understood that the last thing he wanted was for Chad Gregory to see him. If he had his choice, he would never come face to face with Chad again as long as he lived. But here, now, holding his mommy's hand in the middle of the grocery store...it was simply too much.

He ripped his hand away from Allison's, turned around and ran the other way back down the aisle.

"Matthew!" his mom screamed after him. "Matthew, get back here!" She turned and ran after him, terrified of what might happen if he got too far. As she ran past the bank of cash registers, Allison barely noticed the comic books Matthew would never read lying scattered on the linoleum floor. She sprinted outside, into the parking lot, narrowly avoiding slamming into an old man pushing a shopping cart.

She finally caught up to her son, who was pressed up against her car's passenger door, trying repeatedly to pull it open. He was sobbing hysterically as she grabbed him by the shoulders and spun him around to face her.

"Matthew!" she cried, fearful her son was having some sort of nervous breakdown. "Matthew! Matthew, what's wrong with you? What is wrong with you???"

11

That night, after he had calmed down, eaten dinner with his parents, and gone to his room for the night, Matthew laid in his bed, wide awake, for a very long time. In fact, he may not have even gone to sleep at all.

After what had happened at the store, with Matthew running away from his mom and out into the parking lot, Allison made him absolutely promise to keep his gravity boots on all night. Over the last few days, she and Daniel had finally loosened up a little bit, which Matthew had considered a minor victory. But now, his mother's fears had been renewed. "Promise me you won't take them off, Matthew," she had demanded of him. "Swear on your life."

Wanting simply to be by himself, Matthew had agreed. And since he considered swearing on your life to be a very serious promise – he didn't even want to think about what happened to you if you broke it – he kept it, and laid awake, hour after hour, weighed down by the sweaty, uncomfortable boots in his bed.

You see, Matthew had come to a sudden realization when he saw Chad Gregory in the supermarket earlier that day. He had been feeling increasingly uneasy in the days leading up to it, but couldn't quite work out exactly what was wrong. But sometimes, it takes just a single moment for everything to become perfectly clear.

Matthew wanted to go back to the Sky.

He tried to resist this urge, because in a lot of ways, he wanted to *want* to stay on Earth. He wanted to make his parents happy, and he wanted to fit in with the rest of the world. Everything would be so much easier if he could just go about his business of growing up down here on the ground, and find a way to be happy the way he was.

And yet, he knew deep down in his heart that would never be possible. He lifted up the covers, glancing down at his feet clad in their clunky, futuristic black boots, and a sickening feeling flashed through him again. He felt trapped – almost as if he was in some sort of weird prison cell that still allowed him to walk free. Not to mention his parents, nervously hovering over him every waking second. This was no way for any of them to live, a fact that the day's events made painfully obvious.

Seeing Chad in the store represented everything that was wrong with Matthew's life before he left. It wasn't simply a matter of standing up for himself, or trying to somehow overcome the obstacle of his floating. He didn't want to overcome it; he wanted to embrace it. Even if there was no Chad, there would always be something to remind him that he didn't belong here on Earth...and that there was someplace where he did belong.

"I miss it," Matthew whispered to himself in the dark. "I miss the Sky." He took a deep breath, admitting to his own heart what it did not necessarily want to hear: "I need to go back."

12

Now that he had made his decision to return to the Sky, there still remained the small matter of informing his parents. And as you might imagine, the news that Matthew would be leaving again – forever, in all likelihood – would probably not go over too well. This wasn't going to be easy, to say the least.

Matthew walked downstairs the morning after staying up all night coming to this conclusion, his gravity boots feeling even heavier than they usually did. It was Saturday, and Daniel and Allison were in the kitchen, helping each other make breakfast.

"Hey buddy!" Matthew's dad greeted him with a smile. "How many bacon strips do you want?"

"Something to drink?" offered his mom. "There's fresh squeezed orange juice in the fridge."

"No, thank you," Matthew said softly. "Actually, I have something I need to talk to you about."

"Uh oh," grinned Daniel, flipping bacon in the pan. "This sounds serious."

"It is," replied Matthew. That got his parents' attention. A chill fell over the room, as their posture stiffened and they both turned towards their son, giving him their undivided attention.

"What is it, Matthew?" his mother stammered. "What's going on?"

"Well," Matthew began, "there's no easy way to say this, so I'm just going to blurt it out." He took a deep breath, gathering up all the courage he had inside him. "I've...I've decided to go back to the Sky."

There was a long silence. Matthew's parents stared at him, each trying to figure out if this was some sort of cruel joke. When they could not,

Daniel went ahead and demanded, "Is this some sort of cruel joke?"

Matthew shook his head slowly but confidently. "No," he said. "It's not. I'm going back."

Allison instantly became very upset – angry, even. "Matthew, why would you say something like this to us? After everything we've been through, why would you do this to us?" Daniel put his hand on his wife's arm, trying to calm her rising voice, which did not work. "Answer me!" she snapped, louder now. "Why would you say something like that?!"

"Mom, please," said Matthew quietly. "I'm not doing this to hurt you. I love you both very much. It's not that."

"What is it then, Matthew?" asked Daniel, trying to understand. "Why would you want to leave again? What haven't we given you to make you want to stay?"

"I don't belong here, Dad. Since I've been back, it's been...difficult. These boots...." He looked down at the gravity boots he had quickly returned to loathing over the past few weeks. "These boots are like having an oxygen tank underwater. They allow me to live in a world I'm not meant for, just like an oxygen tank lets you swim around under the ocean. But you can't live in the ocean. Sooner or later, you have to get out and go back to where you're meant for." He paused, looking from his dad to his mother. "And I was meant for the Sky. I'm a Nubivagant."

Allison tried to calm herself down, for she was breathing heavily, becoming very upset. "Matthew, honey," she said, sitting down in a chair next to where he was standing. "You haven't been home long enough. Just give it some more time. You'll get used to it, you'll see. I promise you will."

"No I won't, Mom," said Matthew, tears forming in his eyes as well. "I've been through this, before I left. You guys are the only reason I would want to stay here. But I'm afraid..." He stopped, not wanting to say what he needed to say, because he knew how badly it would hurt the two people he loved more than anything.

"It's not enough," Daniel said quietly, sparing him. Matthew looked at his father, tears streaming down his face, and nodded.

Matthew was right. It was difficult for them to hear. Allison shook her head, unable to accept what her son was saying. "But we'll never see you again!" she cried. "It's only by the grace of God that you're here with us now!"

"Exactly," Matthew said. "Don't you see, Mom? The fact that I came back at all...that I'm here with you now...that's a gift from God. You said it yourself: everything happens for a reason. And my reason for being here has come and gone." He took her hand, forcing her to look into his eyes. "You know now. After all this time. You know I'm okay."

Daniel and Allison stared at their son, his words hitting them hard. But in that moment, something amazing happened: they got it. They understood the amazing fortune they had been blessed with, to be able to live the rest of their lives without having to mourn their son anymore. They also understood that keeping Matthew on Earth would be selfish; it would satisfy their happiness at the expense of his.

"You have to live your life," Daniel said, hugging his boy tightly. "You can't live ours. We have no idea what it must feel like to be you. Who are we to stop you?"

The three of them clutched each other and cried for a good long while. Then, as the tears eventually started to die down, there was a long silence. "Well," Allison finally asked, sniffling. "How much longer do we have you for?"

13

It was a very interesting question. If you knew you were leaving your family – your entire planet, in fact – possibly forever...how long would you need to say goodbye?

Perhaps you would make a list of all the things you've ever dreamed of doing, and stay as long as it took to do them. In Matthew's case, he had dreamt of several things he looked forward to doing at some point – drive a car, for example. Visit the pyramids of Egypt, and the Great Wall of China. And for some reason, he had always had this strange fantasy of eating a hot dog pizza (but could never find one on the menu at any of the pizza places he had ever been).

The trouble with a list such as this, Matthew quickly discovered, is that it can take quite a while to tick off every one of your goals. Years, in fact. And when you know you have something difficult to do – such as saying goodbye to people you love – it's often better to get it over with quickly, rather than drag it out. The extra days, weeks, or even months would only serve to weigh heavier and heavier on both Matthew and his parents, so he wouldn't even get to truly enjoy the time he had left on Earth.

That's why Matthew decided he would only spend one more day with his parents. Being a few years away from getting his driver's license, he would simply have to let that dream go. And he could still potentially see the pyramids and Great Wall – just not from the view most people usually see them. However, there was one thing on his list he *could* accomplish in his final day. He could have a hot dog pizza.

Leading up to that glorious Last Supper – a meal his mother assured him would be relatively easy to produce – Matthew simply spent a wonderful last day with his mom and dad. They went out for ice cream.

Matthew and his father played catch with a football in the park, while Allison took pictures she would treasure forever. They came home and sat in the living room together, drinking hot chocolate, talking, laughing, and crying together. It was a beautiful, happy, emotional day none of them would ever forget as long as they lived.

Then Matthew excused himself and went up to his room to do something very important. He sat down at his desk, took out a piece of paper and a pen, and began to write:

"To the parents of Pete & Liam…"

Matthew had been wrestling with the idea of informing the other Nubivagants' parents of their children's whereabouts. He had already broken his oath not to make contact with people on the ground, of course, so he didn't want to do any further damage. But after seeing how relieved his own parents had been by their reunion, and thinking about how terrible Liam felt about his and Pete's departure…he felt he owed it to their mom and dad to ease their suffering.

In fact, Matthew wrote letters to each of the Nubivagants' parents. He told them who he was, how he was just like their children, and his story of meeting them in the Sky. Most importantly, he assured them their kids were alive and well. And even if they never saw them again, he hoped his words could provide them some comfort.

When he was finished, he put each letter in its own envelope and wrote the name of each friend on them. Then he brought them downstairs, handed them to his mom, and told her how important it was to find the Nubivagants' parents and deliver the letters.

His mom teared up, beyond proud of how thoughtful her son was. "Don't worry, sweetie," she said, clutching the letters to her chest. "I'll make it my life's mission."

"Who's getting hungry?" Daniel asked, coming into the kitchen as the sun began going down.

Matthew nodded eagerly. "Starving!"

"Okay," Allison said, putting the letters in a drawer. "I'll order the pizza. Extra large. Just plain cheese, or you want anything else on it? Besides hot dogs, of course."

Matthew considered this important question. It was to be his last Earthly meal, so these details were not to be taken lightly. "Hmmm..." he said, scratching his head. "Maybe throw some pepperoni on there too. Oh! And how about one half with pineapple?"

"Excellent choice," grinned his dad, also getting up. "I'll go throw the dogs on the grill."

Matthew smiled. Then he too stood up, picked up his jacket and put it on. "There's one more thing I want to do before I go," he informed his parents. "I'll be back in a bit."

"What is it?" asked his mom, curious. "I can take you."

"I'll tell you later," he replied mysteriously. "It's just something I need to go do by myself. It won't take long."

"Matthew," his dad said, furrowing his brow. "We've only got you for another few hours. We want to squeeze every last second out of you while you're here!"

"I know, Dad," Matthew said. "I'll be back soon." He smiled at his parents reassuringly. "Trust me."

***

As Matthew walked along the sidewalk in his gravity boots, he closed his eyes and breathed deeply, trying to savor the smells of the trees lining the streets, the sounds of cars driving by, and dogs barking...little things he may very well never experience again.

He tried not to think too much about his decision to leave, but found it was kind of impossible. Whenever you decide to change your life in as dramatic a fashion as Matthew was doing, your mind can start playing tricks on you. You might second-guess yourself, and question if it's really the right thing to do. However, often times, if you stay true to yourself and what you believe is right, then you'll have confidence that you are making the right decision, even if it comes with difficulty and pain. For Matthew, this was one of those times.

But before he said goodbye to his parents, to his life on the ground, there was one bit of unfinished business he felt he needed to take care of. One last little loose end he wanted to tie up. You might argue he didn't actually *need* to do it. But he definitely wanted to. It would give him a sense of closure, which is something people find can be a very useful thing to help them move on from certain unhappy experiences as they go through life.

As Matthew's gravity boots strode through the entrance of the supermarket, it was this feeling of closure he was looking to achieve.

14

Chad Gregory was busy stocking shelves. Specifically, he was transferring crates of bottled water from a large flatbed cart, one by one, to the shelves of aisle 7, which was where one could find all sorts of water products: still water, sparkling water, flavored water, flavored sparkling water, mineral water, tonic water, and even flavored mineral tonic water. It was a task that took a great deal of time, and one Chad found very boring.

But what's even more boring than performing a boring task is *watching* someone perform a boring task. And that was exactly what Matthew was doing. He was standing at the far end of the aisle, making sure Chad couldn't see him by hiding behind a display of potato chips and peeking out from behind it. From this position, he watched Chad, breathing dumbly through his mouth, mindlessly stock water crates onto the shelves for a good fifteen or twenty minutes.

Finally, Chad placed the last of the water bottles onto the shelf. He wiped his brow, which was dotted by a layer of sweat, stood up, and proceeded to wheel the empty cart back down the other end of the aisle, towards the back of the grocery store. That's when Matthew stepped out from behind the potato chip display and began quietly following him.

Completely unaware someone was tracking his movements, Chad lazily pushed the cart past a store manager (to whom he grunted a greeting of some sort) and through two large swinging doors, into the back of the store, where all the extra products were kept. This was the part of the grocery store customers were not supposed to be in. But that didn't stop Matthew from following Chad right through those doors.

He trailed behind Chad as he guided the cart down a hallway, eventually reaching a wall that contained dozens more crates of water. He began to load the cart again, picking up a crate of lemon-lime flavored mineral water, when he noticed Matthew standing about ten feet away, watching him intently.

"You're not supposed to be back here," he said, standing up straight to confront this trespasser. Matthew said nothing. "Hey," Chad said more forcefully, walking towards Matthew now, "I said you're..." He stopped dead in his tracks. His eyes went wide. The crate of water fell from his hands onto the floor with a dull clunk. "It's you," he said softly.

"That's right," Matthew said quietly. "It's me." He began walking slowly towards his former bully, who just stared stupidly at him. *He must have heard the news*, Matthew thought. *He must know I've come back.* But whether or not Chad had indeed known this, it didn't stop him from being too surprised – and perhaps a little scared – to move.

"H-hold it," he said, taking a step back. "Don't come any closer."

Matthew ignored his warning, walking right up to him. Evidently, Matthew had gone through a bit of a growth spurt in the time he had been away, and was now roughly the same size Chad was.

"You're a freak," Chad said, his voice betraying his nervousness. "You're not real. You're a ghost or something. I saw you. You floated away, up into the air."

"Yes, I did," replied Matthew calmly. "And now I'm back."

"How? Why?" Chad swallowed. "What do you want with me?" Matthew slowly bent over, unbuckling one gravity boot, then the other.

"I just wanted to drop by," he explained, standing back up and looking Chad in the eyes, "to say hello." With that, he quickly stepped out of the boots and grabbed Chad by his shirt around the collar with both hands.

"Hey!" Chad protested. "Get your—" But an instant later he was screaming with fright, as both of them rose straight up into the air. "Put me down!" he shrieked, terrified. "Put me down you freak! Oww!!!" He winced in pain as his head hit the ceiling, making a dent in the flimsy tile.

"Here's a little piece of advice," Matthew said coldly. "Stop picking on people. They might be weird, or strange, or different. But they have the abilities to be more special and significant than you will ever be. "

"Okay!" Chad cried, his face red and streaked with tears. "Okay, I'm sorry! I won't pick on anybody! Now put me down, will you? Put me down, please!"

"No problem," Matthew grinned. He pushed Chad away and let go. The bully screamed as he fell fifteen feet through the air, landing right in a garbage can filled with old fruit. The garbage can tipped over, and the next thing he knew, Chad was splayed out on the supermarket floor, covered in gooey, smelly, rotting avocados and banana peels, the garbage can suction cupped to his butt. Still screaming, he rolled around, making a tremendous mess, before finally detaching himself from the can and scrambling to his feet, slipping on all the splattered fruit around him.

Then he looked up at Matthew one last time, who was watching this whole spectacle play out with great amusement. Matthew smiled down at Chad. "Boo," he said.

This time it was Chad who took off running as fast as he could, screaming at the top of his lungs, through the double doors, back down aisle 7, and out the front of the grocery store, to which he would never return.

Matthew, meanwhile, simply propelled himself off the ceiling to the shelving units, then nimbly climbed back down to the ground. He calmly put his gravity boots back on, stepped around the fruity mess, and walked out of the store and back to his house like a perfectly normal teenaged boy, the highly satisfying feeling of closure creating a grin on his face he couldn't have gotten rid of if he'd tried.

15

Matthew's "Last Supper" would be remembered as the most wonderful meal he would ever have. The pizza – extra large, pepperoni, half pineapple – was delivered piping hot from Luigi's, the most famous Italian restaurant in all of Tiburon. Then Daniel added his expertly grilled pieces of 100% all-beef hot dogs on top to create Matthew's lifelong dream: the hotdog pizza.

The three of them sat around the kitchen table, gorging themselves, in utter disbelief that this was not a menu item in every restaurant in the country. Their conversation was surprisingly jovial, filled with laughter. Matthew had his parents howling with his retelling of his encounter with Chad Gregory earlier that day.

"You did *not!!!*" his mom squealed, when Matthew told them about how he had sent Chad racing off in terror by simply saying "Boo" from fifteen feet up in the air.

"Yup," Matthew said. "I actually wish I had thought of something cooler to say – like a catchphrase, or something – but 'boo' just sort of popped out of my mouth."

"And he just ran off screaming?" his dad asked, wiping tears of laughter away from his eyes.

"Yeah. Well, he stumbled around a little in the fruit first," Matthew said, sending the table into a whole new fit of giggles. "I've never seen anybody actually slip on a banana peel. I thought that was only in cartoons."

As the meal was winding down, after everyone had stuffed themselves silly, Daniel raised his glass of red wine. "I'd like to propose a toast," he said. "To our son, Matthew. The most unique person the world has ever known. May you live out the rest of your life in complete happiness, up there in this wonderful place I can only imagine." He paused, getting choked up. "We're so proud of you, buddy. And your mom and I..." He had to stop again, as he was getting very emotional. But Allison took over, finishing his thought.

"We're just so grateful you came back," she said. "We're so lucky we got to see you again. And don't you worry about us. We'll be just fine knowing you're up there, looking down on us." She took a breath, taking Matthew's hand and squeezing it. "And knowing you're happy."

A few moments later, the front door of the Mitchell home opened, and onto the porch stepped Daniel, followed by Allison and Matthew. The three of them strode silently down the driveway to the sidewalk. They turned and looked at each other, none of them quite sure how to say this kind of goodbye.

Daniel looked around. There was no one out on their little street. It was August, and the sun had stayed out as late as it could. But with its light now fading and a bird chirping somewhere, it was as peaceful as could be. "Well," he said. "I guess you'd better take off before someone comes along and sees you floating away. I don't feel like having to explain that."

They all chuckled. Then Matthew took his parents by their hands, looking into their eyes. Their faces were aged and weary, yet peaceful. "Mom. Dad," he said. "I just want to say I'm sorry."

"You have nothing to be sorry for, honey," his mother said. "We understand. We're sad, of course. We're heartbroken. But we understand."

"No," Matthew said. "I'm sorry for getting upset with you, the night before I left. I'm sorry I blamed you for the way I am. And I'm so sorry for the things I said to you. I didn't mean them. I thought I would be able to come home that day and tell you this then, but..." He trailed off, becoming emotional, over a year of pent-up guilt seeping out of him. "I've felt so awful about that night for so long."

"Come here," Daniel said, pulling him in tight to his chest. "Let that

go, you hear me? You have nothing to feel badly about anymore."

"I love you guys so much," Matthew said, tears staining his parents' clothes.

"We know you do," Allison said. "We love you too. More than anything."

"So much," added Daniel. "Always and forever."

After another moment of savoring their final embrace, Matthew finally stepped back, wiping his eyes. "Well," he said heavily, "I guess this is it."

His parents nodded. He knelt down and unlatched the buckles on his boots, then stood up, taking his mom and dad by the hand. He stepped one foot, then the other, out of his gravity boots. And then, slowly at first, he began rising gently into the still summer air, his parents' grasp on his fingers gently slipping away.

Daniel and Allison craned their necks upwards, straining to hold a vision of their child for as long as they possibly could, as he glided peacefully up into the air. When his parents faded from view, Matthew looked up and closed his eyes, gaining speed as the chilly evening breeze rushed past his ears. He noticed the familiar crispness of the thinning air entering his lungs as he ascended through the atmosphere.

To his parents down below, backlit by the beautiful orange and pink of the summer sunset, Matthew Mitchell became but a speck against the Sky.

He was going home.

THE END

EPILOGUE

Matthew arrived right smack in the midst of one of those glorious Sky sunsets. He landed in a big, billowy bank of clouds, immediately enveloped with its cool softness, its pure freshness, that he didn't realize he had missed so much until the instant he returned.

He took a moment to savor his surroundings, then looked around. Off in the distance, he was delighted to see Calvin, Pam, Liam, Pete and Antonella running around, sliding across the great fluffy field of white – the picture of pure happiness. Matthew got to his feet, a smile spreading across his face, and began jogging towards them.

In the time he had spent back on the ground, Matthew often imagined what it would be like to reunite with his best friends, the Nubivagants. He imagined hugging them, laughing with them again, telling them all about the adventure of riding the lightning into the bay, about seeing his parents again, about his decision to ultimately return to them up here in the Sky.

Never did he consider his arrival back in this paradise would be anything other than happy. But as he ran towards the others, and one by one they turned and saw him, their joyous expressions darkened into angry scowls...and it dawned on him that he may have been very, very wrong.

Matthew's run slowed to a trot, then a walk as he eventually reached a distance close enough to the others to speak to them. He stopped altogether, taking in their unhappy faces. They all stared at each other for a long, dreadful moment, a chill running up Matthew's spine that was not from the altitude. Finally Calvin, still the Nubivagants' leader, broke the silence.

"Well, well," he said menacingly. "Look who's back."

ABOUT THE AUTHOR

Ethan Furman is a human male born in San Francisco and residing in Los Angeles. He enjoys daydreaming and creating worlds, often at the same time. This is his first book.

Made in the USA
Middletown, DE
17 April 2018